"You're saying that for Lexi's sake, you'd risk being used for sex?" Leon asked.

It wasn't like that, she told herself. It wasn't just sex. Maybe that was his attitude to her at the moment, but she'd convince him of her innocence, and then his feelings would change.

It was a huge gamble. But worth going for.

"If that's the price," she mumbled crossly.

Her gaze was fixed with unlikely intensity on the floor. The atmosphere burned around Emma as, presumably, Leon battled to stop himself laughing out loud.

"Agreed," he said when she'd abandoned all hope of an answer.

GREEK TYCOONS

**They're the men who have everything—
except a bride...**

Wealth, power, charm—what else could a
heart-stoppingly handsome tycoon need?
In the GREEK TYCOONS miniseries you
have already been introduced to some
gorgeous Greek multimillionaires who are
in need of wives.

Now it's the turn of favorite author Sara Wood,
with her attention-grabbing romance
The Kyriakis Baby.

This tycoon has met his match, and he's decided
he *has* to have her...*whatever* that takes!

Sara Wood

THE KYRIAKIS BABY

GREEK TYCOONS

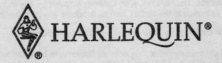

HARLEQUIN®

TORONTO • NEW YORK • LONDON
AMSTERDAM • PARIS • SYDNEY • HAMBURG
STOCKHOLM • ATHENS • TOKYO • MILAN • MADRID
PRAGUE • WARSAW • BUDAPEST • AUCKLAND

My thanks to Maria Doumas for all her help,
and to Richie and Heidi for providing me
with the essential element of my research on little Lexi—
my two-year-old granddaughter Hannah!

ISBN 0-373-12216-0

THE KYRIAKIS BABY

First North American Publication 2001.

Visit us at www.eHarlequin.com

Printed in U.S.A.

PROLOGUE

EMMA sat staring into space, her eyes huge with fear. Her solicitor would come, she told herself. He'd have the answer. He must.

The question wouldn't go away. It was driving her mad. Over and over again it hammered into her aching head.

Where is my baby?

She broke her numb silence with a whimpering moan of despair, a thin, poignant figure drawn in on herself, a woman lost in her own dark world.

Only two weeks ago, she'd stood petrified with fear in the dock and had heard the foreman of the jury pronounce her guilty. It had all been a blur from then on. At Leyton Women's Prison, a note had been handed to her from her brother-in-law, Leon. It had been brutal in its simplicity. 'I have your child.'

She'd heard nothing since. Her baby, Alexandra, had vanished off the face of the earth.

From that moment on, life had been suspended for Emma. Perhaps she had eaten at some time—she wouldn't know. And sleep had come only when her exhausted body could take no more of the waking hell. Even then she'd been plagued by nightmares from which she'd woken sobbing, and drenched in a cold sweat.

That morning, preparing for visiting time, she'd noticed with sudden shock that the months of stress had etched a network of fine lines around her mouth. Furrows scoured her high forehead and a deep notch had been excavated between her brows.

Leon had done this to her.

In the cheap mirror she'd seen that her blonde hair was

5

now lank instead of thick and lustrous. Emma had grimaced, had scraped the lifeless hanks back into a severe pony-tail and had fastened them carelessly with a rubber band, unconcerned that spikes of hair stuck out at all angles.

She looked awful. So what? Who was there to see? She just didn't care. Nothing mattered any more. How could it? Alexandra was her baby and she'd been spirited away. And she was just *six months old*.

Her baby. The focus of her entire existence. Something miraculous, salvaged from a terrible marriage to Taki. Sweet, dimpled little Lexi, whose chuckles and sunny nature could make her smile despite her worries and who'd roused in her such a fierce and tender passion that she'd been shaken by its profundity.

And now Lexi had disappeared. Sitting disconsolately at her appointed place, she took a dog-eared photo from her pocket and stared at it with empty eyes.

Her thoughts tortured her. What happened, she wondered miserably, when a baby was abruptly parted from its mother? Would she eat? Would her child be bewildered and upset— or would anyone's arms, anyone's smile be acceptable? She thought of Lexi, sick from crying, and groaned.

'Oh, my baby!'

She lifted a frail hand to stifle a sob. The action made her vaguely aware that people were stirring around her, their voices rising above the normal subdued mutter that was normally adopted in the large visitors' hall.

Dragged from her inner torment, she lifted her head and gloomily followed the source of interest. And instantly she froze, transfixed by the man who stood in the distant doorway.

Not her solicitor. Someone tall, dark and broad and undeniably Greek, his sharply tailored city suit and impeccable grooming quite incongruous amid the plethora of T-shirts, jogging pants and designer trainers.

Leon. The unfeeling brute who'd abducted her baby.

The pain in her chest intensified as a harsh protest scraped its way from her throat. He'd come to gloat! To read her the riot act, to talk about her lack of morals and his right to take Alexandra.

Right! she seethed. What about her right to justice? Her rights of motherhood? Why had she automatically lost *her* rights as a human being?

Battle-ready, Emma drew her weary body upright, her eyes glittering with anger. She'd have him arrested! He was a fool to have come...

The thudding of her heart seemed to trip and falter as logic poured cold water on her impetuous thoughts. Leon was no fool. If he was here, it was to say something important. What could that be?

Her fevered imagination quickly provided answers. Her baby was dead. A cot death. An accident. An unidentified sickness...

She gasped, and somehow she was on her feet, catapulted by an unknown force that had flung her chair violently to the ground. Leon's eyes swerved to meet hers and he recoiled in shock, as if her appearance appalled him. But Emma was way beyond personal pride.

'*Is she dead?*' she yelled hysterically across the vast hall.

Aghast, he shook his head and mouthed one word. 'No!'

She swayed, her whole body sagging in relief. A warder roughly ordered her to sit but her knees were already giving way beneath her and if a fellow prisoner hadn't righted her chair Emma would have collapsed in a crumpled heap onto the floor.

Her baby was alive. *Alive!* 'Thank you, God. Thank you,' she whispered emotionally.

She trembled all over, her knees juddering against the low metal table. Hands as shaky as a drug addict's covered her eyes. She knew she couldn't take much more.

I must stay calm, she thought in panic. To be more controlled and rational. OK, maybe restraint had seldom featured in her impulsive and passionate nature and her life had been splattered with spectacular foot-in-mouth mistakes—but she had to find some semblance of control. Leon must be persuaded to surrender Lexi.

All her instincts were urging her to hurl abuse and accusations at Leon, to repeat the terrible things she'd privately called him over the past nightmare days. After that, she thought grimly, it would be a nice twist to get him thrown in jail.

But a rare caution warned her against this. He held the welfare of her baby in his hands. Perhaps only he knew where Lexi was. If she annoyed him, she might never see her daughter again.

Her bitter scowl of disappointment would have unnerved him if he hadn't been engrossed in talking to a warder. She glared. Surrounded by grey and depressed people, he looked indecently fit and vigorous as he finished his conversation and threaded his way carefully between the seated prisoners and their visitors.

It seemed to Emma that his whole manner suggested he was concerned that any contact with them might contaminate him irrevocably with some vile disease.

Yes, she thought, near to choking with indignation, this place is a terrible dump! The atmosphere is rank, the bare walls are grimmer than Alcatraz and the clank of keys and clang of gates are two of the most chilling sounds on earth! And she, sweet heaven, she would have to suffer it every wretched day of her life for the next five years!

The injustice made her head spin. She was innocent. *Innocent!*

Aching with anger she tortured herself with the milestones she could miss in five years of little Lexi's life. Her baby's first words, her first steps, the momentous day when she'd start school. And daily cuddles. Smiles, gurgles, small loving arms...

She gave a shuddering sob. Those joys were her right as

a mother! This was her baby, her very flesh and blood, and the person she cared for above all others. How dared he play hide-and-seek with her child!

Resolutions scattered. Uncontainable fury brought her to her feet again when he had come to a mere yard or two's distance of her trembling figure.

'Where is my baby? What have you done with her?' she demanded fiercely.

'Sit down.' Leon snapped.

His outstretched hand gave an imperious wave and, to her amazement, it halted the two frowning warders bearing down on her. Authority, she thought with glowering resentment. He has it in spades. Well, not with me!

'Answer my question, damn you!' she insisted grimly, remaining on her feet out of sheer cussedness.

Tense, and smouldering with a volcanic ferocity, Leon slid into the seat at her table. And yet even there he still managed to dominate the room, perhaps because when seated his height and breadth seemed more than that of the average man. Emma scowled. Nothing about the handsome Leon could ever be remotely termed average.

The blue-black of his hair was more intense, the density of his dark and expressive eyes more mesmerising than any she'd ever seen. The people who met him were always disturbed, intimidated or attracted, depending on their sex and their connection with him. But no one ever forgot the charismatic Leon Kyriakis.

And nor had she. Not one moment of their lovemaking. Despite everything, she felt his inexorable sexual pull now and wilted at the sheer strength of his strong-boned and finely chiselled face, and the curl of his electrifyingly sensual mouth that once she'd kissed and tasted so avidly, so lovingly. Until his utterly callous betrayal.

The furnace in her loins fuelled her loathing as his burning eyes captured her gaze. For a second or two a crackling hostility shot between them, heating up the atmosphere till she felt her skin too must be on fire. And then his ink-black eyes silvered with lethal contempt.

'Sit down, Emma,' he repeated harshly, 'or you'll be back in your cell with your knitting and your mug of cocoa and I'll be halfway to the airport.'

Alarmed, she promptly obeyed, her head lowered in anger while she curbed a wealth of tart answers. She could have kicked herself. She'd *known* she had to handle him carefully. And yet she'd stupidly waded in with all guns blazing. Not much of a kid-gloves approach, was it?

Calm. Restraint. Operate brain before mouth. But how, when violent emotions constantly erupted within her? She missed her baby desperately and her greatest fear was that Lexi might be pining too. No one else knew her little ways. Nobody could understand her baby as she could.

Tears suddenly blurred her vision. Knuckling them away miserably, she looked up with dead, hopeless eyes, all the agony in her heart showing plainly on her ashen face.

'I can't bear this any longer! If you have a shred of pity, you must tell me! Where is my baby?' she implored.

Leon immediately edged his chair back, frowning down at the table. 'Safe.'

He cleared his throat and fiddled with his cuff, apparently annoyed that it was showing a centimetre less than its twin.

'Thank God,' she whispered.

She swallowed ineffectively. There was a solid lump blocking her throat and she gagged on it, desperate to clear it so she could speak. Seeing this, he pushed a glass of water towards her and she stared, oddly surprised at the contrast between their two hands.

His was tanned, broad and virtually pulsing with life. Hers looked a ghastly white, just skin and bone, as if, she thought deliriously, she was in a living death.

She clasped the glass as if grabbing a lifeline but her hand shook too much when she raised it and she abruptly put it back on the table. No histrionics. Reasoned argument. For her baby's sake...

The hard lump eased a little and she could swallow. 'How...how is she?'

Her voice quavered and his mouth immediately contracted into a hard line. What had she said to annoy him? Emma felt awash with terror in case he lost his not inconsiderable temper and refused to listen to her.

'Don't do this to me. I must know,' she begged wretchedly.

'Alexandra is well and happy.'

He spoke in a stiff undertone and she leaned far across the table, frantic to hear every word he uttered. Leon seemed to shrink back as if she was invading his space. He loathed her, she thought dully. How was she to win him round?

She bit her soft lower lip intently, anxious to hear about her beloved baby. 'Is she very upset? Does she...cry much?' she said jerkily.

'No.'

Her eyes widened. 'Don't lie to me!' She flung the words at him. 'She must!'

'If I say she doesn't, then it's true,' he answered irritably. 'She'll cry for a while when she's tired or hungry or needing comfort but she soon stops. Otherwise she's content. I am not a liar. I come from an honest people,' he pointed out, forcing the words fiercely through his tightly clenched teeth.

'I'm honest too. I don't deserve to be in prison, accused of fraud,' she hurled.

'Such injustice.' He tutted, his expression cynical and disbelieving.

Emma realised that it was no use trying to persuade him that she was whiter than snow. He had her down as a criminal and that was that.

'Lexi's OK, then?' she persisted in a plaintive tone. 'She's eating properly?'

'How many times do I have to tell you?' he said irritably.

'She's absolutely fine. Use your common sense. Why would I allow any harm to come to her?'

Emma paused to consider this. In her experience Greeks loved children and had a way with them. Lexi was probably being spoiled rotten.

A twinge, as sharp as a knife, twisted in her breast with such force that her hand lifted to ease it. For her daughter's sake she felt relieved that all was well, but she felt more bereft than ever.

Maybe she wasn't necessary to Lexi's well-being at all. Her child could exist without her. But could she exist without her child? Her heart went cold and she shuddered, sliding her thin arms around her shivering body, consoling herself with the fact that only she knew all the tiny things that made Lexi truly content.

'She does have her teddy bear, doesn't she?' she began shakily. 'And I don't suppose you realise that she needs her yellow blanket—'

'It's with her as we speak. I removed everything from your house which looked remotely as if it belonged to Lexi,' he retorted.

Emma gaped, astounded at his thoroughness. 'You planned this!' she accused hotly. 'You knew exactly what you would do if the jury pronounced me guilty—'

'Of course I did. I couldn't allow my late brother's child to remain in the care of a stranger,' he snapped.

'She's my neighbour. Lexi knows her. It was only temporary, anyway,' she argued. 'I fully expected to be free—'

'And what did you organise if not?' he asked sardonically.

'If there was a problem, my neighbour was to bring her to the mother-and-baby unit here.'

He still hadn't answered the question. Where was her daughter? Suddenly she had a flash of fear, picturing her baby abandoned outside in a car, or in her buggy by the prison entrance where anyone could abduct her... She drew in a choking breath.

'And what about *your* babysitting arrangements? If you're here,' she said jerkily, her voice rising in panic, 'who's looking after Lexi now?'

His eyes flickered. 'Marina. My—'

But she'd got there before him. 'Your *wife!*' she said breathily.

Emma sat stunned. Of course. Who else? she thought dully. And then she noticed something strange. There was a sliver of pain knifing across the dark depths of his eyes and bitterness had drawn his mouth into a hard line.

He wasn't happy, she realised with a shock. Pangs of half-remembered love touched her shuttered heart. She'd adored him once. They'd been students together and he'd been everything to her. But one day, totally out of the blue, she'd seen him emerging from a local restaurant with a drop-dead gorgeous blonde on his arm. Her world had disintegrated rapidly.

'An engagement party,' the obliging Greek waiter had said, his apron stuffed with tips from the affluent, laughing crowd.

The lintel above the entrance where they were posing for photographs had born a banner with the elaborately printed legend, Leon and Marina. It had been emblazoned with hearts and love knots. The waiter picked up a discarded menu with the same design and the appalled Emma had known that this must have been planned for some time.

Tears of rage and misery had rendered her speechless. He'd been organising his wedding while vowing he loved her...even while he was sleeping with her!

'Leon!' she'd cried rawly.

He'd looked directly at her and turned a deathly white. *'Emma!'*

All eyes had been upon her then. Clearly appalled that she'd found him out, he'd spoken to a younger man at his side who'd come over and introduced himself as Leon's brother, Taki.

'He's the Kyriakis heir, she's the Christofides heiress,' Taki had explained gently as he'd driven her home. 'Our families have been linked for generations. Don't take this personally,' he'd said soothingly, when she'd continued to sob. 'It's how we do things. We need sex so we find a woman who is amenable. Then we marry a more suitable virgin.'

The humiliating words dug deep. She'd been used as a whore! Bought presents, taken out to dinner...and in return he'd pillaged her heart and soul and body!

Broken-hearted, her self-esteem at rock bottom, she'd relied increasingly on the attentive, kind Taki. His respect for her had been deeply touching. Eventually she'd succumbed to Taki's charm offensive and married him, unaware of his fatal need to outdo his rival brother.

She gave a grimace. Incredibly, Taki had believed that Leon would be jealous of his marriage to her. But why, when she had nothing—and the elegant, shopaholic Marina had breeding, wealth and social position?

Her heart thudded in alarm. This was the woman who was now looking after her child! What, she thought with uncharacteristic sourness, did a clothes-horse on legs know about such things?

Her brows beetled together in a fierce scowl. 'Your wife had better be the Mary Poppins of child care—or you'll have me to reckon with!' she muttered.

'Marina has a daughter of her own,' he drawled crushingly.

She felt she'd been stabbed in the lungs. Leon had a child. 'Bully for you both,' she cried, finding her breath again. 'Then, you don't need mine.'

'Damn right, I don't.'

Her mouth opened in astonishment. He didn't even want her darling Lexi. 'Then, why take her?' she asked, aghast.

He looked down his patrician nose at her. 'I had no choice.'

'No...*choice*?' She spluttered the words incoherently.

Leon looked grim. 'She needs a home. She needs us.'

'Me. She needs *me*. I'm her mother,' she quavered.

'Not much of one.'

'I'm terrific.'

'Matter of opinion.'

'I'll get out on appeal—'

'I think not. The evidence was clear-cut and damning. Get used to this situation, Emma,' he said sharply. 'Serve your time—'

'I will if I must, unfair though it is. I could bear anything if I had my baby back.'

'Out of the question.'

Incensed, she banged the table and knocked over the glass of water which spilled onto her lap. Leon produced a handkerchief but she refused it, too caught up in her bid for her child to care that her dress was wet through.

'If you're a father,' she said, hoarse with emotion, 'then think how you'd feel if your child was taken from you.'

Astonishingly, his gaze became cynical, as if that wouldn't be hard to bear. He has no heart, she thought bleakly. Her beloved baby wasn't even wanted. How could he feel like that? The only Greek in the world who didn't like children and he had to snatch her baby.

'It's happening all the time,' he observed obliquely. 'People split up, children end up with one of the parents—'

'But I'm the *remaining* parent,' she pointed out, barely clinging to sanity. Why couldn't he understand what Lexi meant to her? She had no one else in the world. 'You have no right to abduct my child. I could have you arrested.'

'That would be extremely unwise,' he said with quiet menace.

She tensed in alarm. 'Why?'

'It wouldn't get your child back.'

'Maybe not,' she muttered bitterly, giving her wet dress a shake, 'but it would bring a big grin to my face and play merry hell with your social life.'

His breath hissed in and he fixed her with eyes as cold as

charity. 'You'd do that to score points off me?' he enquired softly.

Her desolation intensified. Of course not. She'd gain nothing—other than a useless, petty satisfaction—by giving Leon grief. And she'd ruin her chances of finding Lexi.

Her chest seemed to tighten with despair. 'I'd do anything, anything to get my own child back where she rightfully belongs,' she declared jerkily.

There was a lift of a black-winged eyebrow. 'You're at a slight disadvantage being in prison,' he observed.

She flushed, a hectic colour burning two scarlet spots on her pale, bony cheeks.

'Have you no heart? No soul? She should be with me—'

'Alexandra might be legally yours but that's as far as it goes,' he said sternly. 'You just aren't fit to be her mother.'

'That's not fair,' she seethed, outraged at the slur.

'*Fair?* You dare to speak of fairness?' he rasped, his voice shaking with barely contained fury as he struggled to keep the volume down. 'How can you sit there claiming to be as innocent as a Madonna? You systematically defrauded members of my family *and* our lifelong friends and business acquaintances, and left them penniless,' he hissed.

His big fists clenched on the table and she stared at them, suddenly frightened of his intense passion.

'But that's the point—I didn't,' she protested, her voice wobbling alarmingly. 'It...it wasn't me—'

'You disgust me!' he scathed. 'Have you any idea of the consequences of your crime in our close-knit society? Our family bank here in London was seen as the safest place this side of Fort Knox. People relied on us. *Trusted* us. No wonder Taki got drunk! His own wife had destroyed his family business, his family honour and innocent lives. He'd lost his job and his own honour—'

'Honour!' she choked.

'Yes! Ever heard of the word?' he taunted.

'You *hypocrite!*' she said breathily, forgetting Taki's dishonesty and attacking Leon's instead. 'How can you sit there and talk of honour when you forgot to mention your engagement to another woman while we were together?'

That went home. He recoiled as if she'd slapped him, his skin suddenly taut and sickly pale.

'That *was* a matter of honour—'

'Yes, I know. Honouring some long-standing family arrangement,' she said scornfully. 'You used me for sex—and you talk of *honour*.'

'Don't try to wriggle out of this,' Leon retorted, white-lipped. 'The truth is that Taki was appalled at what you'd done. And he got so paralytic that some bastard mugged him and left him to die in the gutter. Your actions caused his death.'

Frozen in horror at Leon's twisted interpretation of the facts, she tried to speak. But his accusation had stunned her with its cruelty and all she could do was to slur helplessly, 'It's a lie! I'm...I'm...'

'Guilty on all counts,' Leon finished in disgust. 'Now, I hope you understand that I feel I owe you no sympathy. My family means everything to me and you ripped it apart with your evil scheming. You destroyed my only brother—'

'No—'

'Are you denying,' he went on relentlessly, 'that you cold-bloodedly married him out of petty revenge—?'

'I loved him—'

'Liar! He said you'd asked for a divorce.'

Emma bit her lip hard. She hadn't wanted to split her family up. But she'd had no choice. Leon knew nothing of the agonising that had gone before her painful decision.

'Y-yes, but—'

'Don't bother to find excuses,' Leon said, growling. 'Taki had served his purpose. You'd seen a way to make me pay for marrying Marina and you took it. Well, congratulations. You succeeded in making my life hell.' His eyes glittered. 'Forgive me,' he ground out through his teeth, 'if I return the compliment.'

She gave a low moan and buried her face in her hands, all

hope virtually abandoned. His Greek heritage made him proud and hot-blooded and deeply devoted to his family. In his eyes, she'd harmed that family. And so he wanted to destroy her. And how better than to take away the baby she adored?

Panic and despair filled her head as defeat stared back at her. But she knew she had to rouse herself and make one last attempt to convince Leon that he'd jumped to all the wrong conclusions.

'You must listen to me,' she begged. 'You've got it all wrong. I've done nothing to be ashamed of. I'm truly innocent—'

'Sure. You, and everyone in here,' he mocked.

'No, I am—'

'You knew what was happening,' he said snarling. 'You were the financial director—'

'That's the point, I wasn't, it was in name only I *swear*—'

'Stop it!' he snapped furiously. 'You've perjured yourself enough.'

'Leon,' she mumbled, 'you're not giving me a chance—'

'Did you give Taki a chance? Or those people who are now living on pittances instead of healthy pensions? My family will have to pull out all the stops to ensure they don't suffer, thanks to you. It could take us years.'

It was hopeless. He was implacable. 'How can we have become such enemies?' she asked miserably. 'Once…'

The rest of her words died in her throat. His eyes blazed with such an intense hatred that every muscle in her body turned to water, her hands feebly clawing at the table for support as she struggled to stay in her seat and not slide to the floor in a boneless heap.

Leon's face suddenly loomed close to hers and she found herself pinned in place by the anguish that ripped at his face.

'Once! Once we were lovers,' he said in a terrible, raw whisper. 'My passion matched yours, my hands caressed your body. My lips knew yours, our bodies pulsed together—'

'Leon—' she said, breathily brokenly, unable to bear any more.

He touched her face, his fingers trembling with a barely contained passion. She assumed it to be a shuddering anger and shrank back in distress.

Leon's nostrils flared. 'I'd never have come within a mile of you if I'd realised the depths of your viciousness—that you could blame Taki for the fraud.'

'It was him,' she insisted hopelessly.

'Pity the jury didn't agree with you,' he countered.

There was a sudden silence between them. They were at deadlock. Emma gave up. Her late husband's betrayal was no longer important.

Alexandra's future *was*. The next few moments could affect her child's life for ever. Sick and weak, she rallied the last drop of energy in her body.

'Shun me,' she declared, her voice shaking with emotion. 'Hate me, think what you like. Forget I ever lived if that pleases you.' Panic rose within her like an uncontrollable flood and she raised a tearful face in one last passionate plea. 'But let me have the child I love.'

'Not in a million years,' he replied coldly. 'I won't let Taki's daughter be brought up in an English prison by a callous, cold-blooded female. She's out of your reach now...not even in this country.'

Abruptly he rose to go. Emma couldn't speak, could barely think for shock. Her beloved Lexi was in Greece! A cracked sound filtered through her trembling lips as the reality hit her like a stone. Her mouth quivered as a terrible emptiness enveloped her. She hadn't a hope of getting her baby back.

The nausea rose to her throat and sweat beaded her forehead. Hardly aware of her surroundings, she struggled for control, afraid that she'd be sick, then and there.

'You're...a *monster*!' she whispered in horror.

'Am I?' he said curtly. 'And what kind of mother are you? Did you once think of Lexi while you were plotting your criminal activities? Did you ever wonder what would happen to her if your fraud was discovered? Were you so wrapped up in your own selfish need for vengeance that it didn't *matter* what happened to any of the people who had the misfortune to be involved in your life?'

Emma gazed at him tearfully. 'But...I love her,' she mumbled.

'And I have her best interests at heart,' he countered grimly. 'She will remain with me. I came to put your mind at rest. Lexi is safe and content and will be well cared for. She will be taught to be honourable, well-mannered and honest.'

It sounded so dutiful. So utterly empty of warmth and affection. This was her baby he was talking about! A child who needed cuddles and affection, a mother's love... 'Is that all?' she said jerkily.

'More than you would have provided,' he said coldly.

'Leon!' she said choking, tears spilling unchecked down her unhappy face as she was forced to accept the unthinkable.

There would be another woman mothering her baby, someone else reading bedtime stories, comforting Lexi, watching her grow up...snuggling into that baby-scented skin...

She gave a shuddering moan. 'Oh, Leon, what about *love*?'

He had half-turned to leave. Taut in every line of his body, he jerked his head around and looked her full in the eyes. Now she was sure of his unhappiness, of some deep pain he suffered.

Her limpid gaze pleaded with him for compassion and understanding. The silence and the tension between them intensified and she knew they were both thinking of the past when they had been wildly happy together and without a care in the world.

'Love,' he rasped with a glacial contempt, 'is a fool's *illusion*.'

CHAPTER ONE

SECURE within the walled grounds of Leon's country mansion, the two-and-a-half-year-old Alexandra slept contentedly in Leon's arms while he laid plans for her to inherit his domain. When, he reminded himself grimly, he'd dealt with the problem of his ex-wife and her child.

He returned to more pleasant thoughts, planning for the day when he'd tell Lexi how his family had been rewarded with land for outstanding bravery. Like his father before him, he'd show his niece the hill where a lookout had spotted the Saracen pirates who'd roamed the seas of Greece in the sixteenth century, and who'd threatened to capture the entire island of Zakynthos.

And they'd walk from the beach where Kyriakis ships had set out for the decisive battle, to the shady, vine-covered terrace where he now sat. There, he would tell her, in his late father's words, that the land would be hers, all the way from the coast, across the fertile plain and to the hills beyond.

She murmured in her sleep and burrowed deeper, her wilful little face soft with dreams. Smiling down at her, he stroked the silky blonde curls and had a sudden, sharply painful recollection of caressing Emma's shining hair long, long in the past.

The rosy image was brutally replaced by Emma's shocking appearance more than two years ago, when he'd confronted her in that unspeakable prison. He shifted, uncomfortable with the memory. In a moment of weakness he'd almost given in to her, his intentions shaken by Emma's distress and her alarming physical deterioration.

But she had shown no penitence and he couldn't ignore the facts. Lexi's moral welfare had been threatened. It had

21

been his duty to protect his brother's child in accordance with his promise to his ailing father.

He looked down as Lexi stirred, her eyes opening to show the same cerulean blue as those of her mother. He smiled fondly. Reluctant to take on another child, he'd nevertheless been enchanted by her.

'Mama,' she whimpered, her face crumpling in bewilderment.

He winced as if from a body blow. 'It's OK. I'm here, sweet pea,' he said softly, holding the tiny body close.

He knew she wasn't properly awake and was likely to sleep for another twenty minutes or so. She was dreaming. At her tender age she couldn't have any memory of a mother who'd last held her when she was still a baby. Could she?

Alexandra curled up grumpily and her eyes closed again, soothed by his stroking hands. But Leon felt disturbed and unsettled.

When she seemed to be safely asleep again he headed for his study where he placed her carefully on a wide sofa at the far end of the room, protecting her with a barricade of pillows.

The house slumbered, silent and hushed. Marina, who was sharing the big house with him still, insisted everyone took a siesta after lunch and he'd often had cause to be grateful for the respite it afforded him.

Frowning hard, he strode up and down, thinking. The moment he'd dreaded was almost upon him. Lexi would soon ask questions about her mother. He needed to know what to say. Or…what to show her.

His eyes slewed to the locked drawer in his desk. Something other than his own will compelled him to stride over and slip the key in the lock. His fingers shook with impatience. Nothing could stop him now, not even the need to protect his own bruised heart.

With his pulses pounding loudly in his ears, he removed the home video from the drawer and slotted it into the machine. After a quick glance at the sleeping Lexi, he pulled up a leather armchair and focussed tensely on the unfolding pictures.

A slow hiss escaped his lips. He'd forgotten how beautiful Emma had been when they'd gone out together. She'd been twenty, studying economics on day-release at the college where he was taking a postgraduate course.

Her sense of fun and *joie de vivre* lit the screen and Leon found himself on the edge of his seat watching avidly as her supple and voluptuous body dipped and swayed in a laughing parody of a belly dancer. Sex oozed from every pore of her body, heating him, tugging at his loins.

Giggling, she ruined the profoundly erotic effect by whooping and turning a series of exuberant cartwheels.

'Mama!'

'Lex!'

Leon jerked around, poleaxed. Alexandra was sitting up and staring wide-eyed at the screen. His heart pounded hard as the hairs stood up on the back of his neck. She didn't know what she was saying.

Cursing himself for being careless, he hit the off button. Lexi scrambled over the cushions and ran to him. Before he knew what she was doing she had reached across his knee and switched the video on again.

'Mama,' she said in firm defiance when he snapped it off for the second time.

He stopped breathing. It was a coincidence. She was copying Marina's child who was always yelling for her mother. Only the other day Lexi had called his ex-wife Mama and had been quickly corrected, only to repeat the word again and again until the edgy Marina had screamed in exasperation.

He smiled wryly, remembering how secretly amused he'd been by his bolshie little niece. Lexi was strong-willed; as stubborn and as determined as any Kyriakis male.

And, he acknowledged, with the added advantage of devastatingly female weapons. Already she'd climbed onto his lap and her arms were twining around his neck pleadingly.

'Lexi see,' she coaxed, showering his face with kisses.

Melting already, he considered this. The damage—if any—had been done. If not, they could both enjoy the remainder of the video. And he wanted to, very much.

Brushing aside the danger to his peace of mind, he nodded. 'All right,' he conceded.

'Thank you very much,' she chanted solemnly, remembering her manners.

He grinned and hugged her. 'Minx,' he murmured fondly, curling up with her to watch.

He could see that Lexi was enraptured by Emma's virtuoso performance for the camcorder. As always, Emma went too far—this time, one cartwheel too many—and to the little girl's delight Emma rolled helplessly into a nearby duck pond before emerging hooting with laughter, her eyes sparkling, pearly teeth glistening and her hair festooned with pondweed.

'Finished,' he announced tautly, when the screen went blank.

His memory furnished the rest. He'd put down the camcorder and dragged Emma into his arms. He'd kissed her till she couldn't breathe. Oh, God, he remembered so well!

Seven years later he could still smell and taste the pondweed and feel the indescribable warmth and softness of her welcoming, laughing mouth as she'd lured him into the woodland beyond.

Grimly he swung Lexi into his arms and suggested a swim, relieved that she had asked no questions. He wasn't ready to supply answers.

As she tugged him along excitedly, he reflected that he would have to decide how he should handle the question of Emma. Did he tell his niece the truth one day about her jailbird mother? Or should he give a sanitised version? And should he ever reveal who the woman in the video was?

His brow furrowed deeply. If he did the latter, Lexi would

be captivated. She'd want to meet her mother—whereas he intended to keep them apart as long as possible.

He felt a chill steal over him despite the heat of the early afternoon. Emma would be released in a couple of years or so. And then Lexi would no longer be safe from harm.

He looked at her sweet face as she sang happily to herself, absorbed in 'helping' her to wriggle into a bathing costume which sported a large daisy cutely adorning her small bottom. His heart lurched. Ever the attentive, doting uncle, he swept her curls up and expertly fastened them with a scrunchie.

He loved this little scrap. From day one she'd wormed her way into his frozen heart and with every flutter of her lashes and big, gummy smile she had set about thoroughly defrosting it. Now she meant everything to him—and life without her would be untenable.

He made a silent pledge. Emma would never get her daughter back. Not while there was still breath in his body.

'And...Mrs Kyriakis,' murmured the smooth, young immigration officer, 'what are your plans now you are on Zakynthos?'

Emma remained composed, even though her heart and stomach seemed to have shot down an elevator into her trainers and were now sending alarm signals through her entire system.

She'd had a lot of practice in self-control over the past two years—and getting into the country was far more important than some of the things she'd silently borne in prison. Consequently she managed to flash a warm smile.

'Simple. I'm going to get a tan!' she announced airily.

With a show of cheerfulness she indicated the sun cream, lodged precariously on top of her belongings which had been tipped unceremoniously out of her case.

'I see. Staying...where?' enquired the officer idly, scanning a list.

She craned her neck. It looked like the names of people.

Her dramatically fertile imagination provided details. Drug dealers and terrorists. Rapists. Paedophiles, whatever. Her heart leapt back into her chest with an unnerving suddenness and sat there palpitating. Maybe she was on that list as an undesirable!

'Your hotel?' prompted her interrogator.

Emma forced another broad smile. 'Hotel! I wish. I'm looking for something cheap. A friend of mine said it was easy to find rooms to rent,' she confided. 'Can you recommend anywhere?'

He studied her thoughtfully and ignored her attempt to disarm him. 'You have a Greek name.'

She'd been ready for that one. Nodding slowly, she gave herself time to calm her leaping nerves and to steady her voice. 'My husband...' she frowned at the shaky delivery but plunged on '...he...he died in England more than two years ago.'

Unfazed by her apparent agitation, the officer gave her a calculating stare. She recognised in him the same detachment as that adopted by the prison officers. They'd heard too many lies and too many sob stories to be anything but suspicious of emotion.

'He has family here?'

Emma tensed. Her solicitor had said there were many people in the phone book with the name Kyriakis and her arrival shouldn't provoke comment. She hoped this officer was merely bored and was using her to hone his interviewing technique.

'My late husband lived and worked in England. His family—wherever they are,' she said, suggesting a vagueness as to the Kyriakis whereabouts, 'were opposed to our marriage. They never came to the wedding.' She allowed a puzzled frown to ripple her forehead. 'What is this? Everything's in order, isn't it? All I want is a holiday in the sun. I've had an operation. I need rest and no hassle—'

'Ah. The pills.'

Emma watched as he curiously fingered the homoeopathic remedies for sickness and exhaustion. Her prison sentence had been cut short on compassionate grounds because she'd been so ill. She had her solicitor to thank for that. Dear John! Bless him for his support. She glanced at her watch and bit her lip. He'd be waiting for her, wondering where she was...

'Someone meeting you?'

She blinked. He was good! Someone ought to promote him to head inquisitor, she thought wearily.

'I've never been here before,' she said, evading the question with a politician's skill.

'You looked at your watch.'

'Yes. I need to eat at regular intervals and take my pills at certain times. With the two-hour time difference, I was anxious not to get in a muddle.'

'Really.'

This man would have made an angel edgy, she thought sourly. She felt suddenly weak and passed a hand over her hot forehead.

'I need to sit down,' she muttered. Without waiting for permission she went to a bench against the wall and sank onto it, leaning her back against the cold stone, terrified of failure. 'I don't understand the problem,' she said quietly. 'I can't be the only person who arrives without any definite accommodation. I don't have enough money or clothes to stay here for long, you can see that. I'm not carrying drugs, or anything else illegal. I'm just an ordinary woman hoping for some sun, sea and sand to help me become well.'

Indifferent to her evident frailty, the officer turned over the contents of her case with a desultory hand.

'I see. Would you wait here?' he asked politely.

As if she had any choice! Patiently she waited. An hour. Two. Exhausted from her four a.m. start, she curled up on the hard bench and promptly went to sleep.

'Mrs Kyriakis?' The officer was shaking her shoulder. 'You can go. Enjoy your holiday.'

Relief brought her fully awake. She was free! A joyful smile began its journey across her face but she lowered her sparkling eyes hastily and tried to think how an ordinary holiday-maker would feel.

'About time,' she grumbled. Getting up stiffly, she saw that she'd slept for nearly an hour. 'Some welcome!'

The officer gave an only-doing-my-duty shrug and she continued her show of irritation as she repacked her case then trudged out of the room.

She couldn't believe it. She was here. Really here. And not far away was little Lexi. Soon she'd be holding her baby in her arms again. Excited, Emma thought blissfully of the moment when Lexi would call her Mummy.

'Wonderful!' She breathed ecstatically.

Back in his office, the officer punched numbers on his mobile. 'She's on her way,' he warned.

Leon thanked the officer, tucked his mobile into the pocket of his linen jacket and waited tensely beneath the shade of the tamarisk and pine trees opposite the airport entrance.

The first call, some two hours earlier, had come out of the blue. For a moment he'd thought the officer had made a mistake but the name, the age and the description had been spot on. If this *was* Emma, then the young man's alertness had possibly prevented an attempted abduction.

Leon thrust his shaking hands into his pockets and forced back the flash of fear. A tiny child's happiness depended on his ability to handle this situation. Caught off guard by the unexpectedness of Emma's arrival, he'd had only a short time to decide his plan of action. But he must make no mistake in its execution.

He stiffened, every muscle in his body creaking with strain. His heart raced. It was Emma.

Like a butterfly spreading its wings, she drew herself up, took a deep breath and flung her head back to absorb the sunshine, her whole body language exuding uninhibited joy.

'Entirely misplaced,' he muttered.

If she thought she was free to snatch her daughter, she was wrong! He'd watch her every step of the way. She might be devious and driven by revenge to cause him the maximum amount of trouble, but he was on his home ground and had a whole raft of people looking out for his best interests.

And Lexi's. God keep her safe. How could Emma drag a child away from the only home she'd ever known? Her lawyer, John Sefton, had hinted something like this might happen but he'd never believed she could ignore her daughter's needs so ruthlessly.

Emma set off as if she knew where she was going. Interesting. He kept his distance as she headed for the taxi rank—which she ignored. The drivers didn't ignore her though, and he didn't blame them for staring in admiration.

'*Poli oraya*,' they murmured, seeking his agreement as he drew level to them.

Yes, she was strikingly attractive, he acknowledged grudgingly. Prison had obviously been no hardship and the gaunt, sick woman had become a beauty again.

Her long-legged stride was fluid, giving an impression of suppleness and energy. Leon's mind, perhaps overwhelmed by those lushly swaying hips, translated that vigour into Technicolor visions of athletic sex.

'Forget it. You're celibate,' he muttered under his breath, reluctantly amused by his astonishing arousal.

But he couldn't. She'd gained weight—though not the plumpness of her youth. To Leon's hot appraisal her figure was more spectacular than ever before: full breasted, yet slim, and with a tiny waist above those eye-catchingly seductive hips.

She wore a blindingly blue sundress the same colour as her eyes and her blonde hair swung around her shoulders in a thick and glossy cloud. Her skirt was being whipped by the wind around her long, bare legs and afforded breathtaking glimpses of firm and shapely thighs.

Leon tried to normalise his thudding pulses as she stopped and looked about her—clearly waiting for someone. Caught between desiring and despising her, he allowed himself the brief luxury of letting his sexual imagination run riot.

He wished he hadn't. His libido seemed to be making up for lost time and it was taking over his mind as well as his body.

With hazy eyes, he saw a car come to a stop alongside her. A man clambered out. Emma opened her arms in welcome, her face wreathed in smiles.

Leon's vision sharpened. John Sefton, Emma's lawyer. He knew him well from the custody discussions they'd had over the past two years. And that was no proper greeting between a professional man and his client, he thought darkly. Too much hugging. Too much delight.

Spurred by an anger which had come from nowhere, Leon noted the stubby male fingers gravitating slowly towards Emma's highly touchable rear and strode forwards before the roving hand reached its target.

His heart pounded like a trip hammer in his chest and he had to concentrate hard on containing the overwhelming emotions which battled for supremacy in his seething brain.

'Well! They're letting jailbirds into my country now!' he drawled.

Emma gasped at the venom-laced voice, detached herself from John's enthusiastic embrace and whirled around.

'*You!*' she said stupidly.

Leon's cynical eyes lingered mockingly on her parted lips and she felt a flush creeping up her body as he began to investigate the rest of her with breathtaking thoroughness.

'Yes, me. I live here,' he observed when his tour had climbed to her cleavage. 'What's your excuse?'

She bristled, wanting to shout, My child, dammit! What do you think? Instead, she summoned her new and remarkable self-control, raised an eyebrow and with cool composure murmured, 'I've come to arrange access.'

Custody was out of the question. John had fought for that on her behalf ever since she'd been sent to prison and he'd hit a brick wall. Access was a different matter—though she intended to remove Lexi from the island, once they had got to know one another well.

'I was going to call you. I wanted time with Emma first,' John said to Leon, looking flustered.

'Oh, yes?' Leon drawled coldly and turned to Emma. 'I've got half an hour free. We'll discuss it. Without your boyfriend.'

Emma let her mouth tighten with irritation. 'You've met John several times. You're perfectly aware that he's my legal adviser—'

'And hopes for more,' Leon murmured, his gaze challenging John's.

'Don't be ridiculous—' she protested indignantly.

'Ask him,' drawled Leon.

'My relationship with my client is her own business,' John said rather pompously.

And, she felt, defensively. She looked up at him with different eyes. Could Leon be right? And then she frowned. Of course not! It would suit Leon to cause trouble between herself and John, who'd become her friend and ally.

'John has worked long and hard on my case. He's good and kind and worth ten of you,' she declared loyally. 'Without him I'd have been alone in the world.' Her face flushed when she thought of those terrible, heart-breaking days and her voice faltered. 'John was there for me. He stood by me and encouraged me when I was desperate. And he never gave up fighting for my early release.'

'How dedicated. And, I trust, well-paid?' Leon said purring.

But the look he gave her lawyer was one of pure menace and she felt John shrink back in apprehension. That bothered her. She needed her lawyer to be more than a match for Leon.

'That's none of your business,' she replied. Selling her

house had been a price worth paying. 'The sun is too hot for me. Can we find some shade?' she suggested and slipped in a crafty, 'Or perhaps we could go to your home now?'

Leon's dark eyes considered her for a moment. She met them boldly at first, confident of her hard-won protective shell. But slowly his eyes seemed to melt and she felt as if she was floundering in fathoms-deep water. A silky sensation seemed to be flowing up her body, softening her tense muscles and turning her brain to treacle.

The heat. It was melting her as though she were an ice cream. She licked her dry lips and lifted her hair from her damp neck.

'I will talk to you and you alone,' Leon said, his voice low and rolling through her unnervingly. 'Otherwise... nothing.'

'That's not on, Emma!' John began in protest.

She gave him a particularly dreamy smile, partly because of the warm liquidity of her body and partly because her friendship with John seemed to annoy Leon.

'What does it matter? It's what we want and I'll come to no harm,' she said affectionately. John didn't look too sure. Amused, she rested her hand on his arm and fondly kissed his cheek. 'I'll see you later. I've got your number. I ought to speak to Leon if I'm to visit Lexi before...' she gave him a conspiratorial smile '...before I return to England.'

'I don't like it. Don't make any decisions. Don't agree to anything. Remember his agenda,' John advised sullenly.

'Of course,' she said soothingly. 'I'll—'

'Can we get on?' interrupted Leon irritably.

'We have a man in a hurry!' She smiled at John. 'See you later.'

Leon pointedly opened the door of her lawyer's car but his bad temper didn't disturb her at all. As John drove grumpily away she reflected that this was more than they'd hoped.

Leon's intransigence had been so deeply rooted that she'd thought he'd refuse even to see her. She and John had consequently planned on resorting to the courts for access and they had been resigned to a lengthy legal battle.

In preparation two weeks previously, John had brought in everything she'd need: extra clothes and medication, the dwindling remainder of the money from the sale of the house where she and Taki had lived—and a selection of toys and clothes for Lexi.

But now Leon was agreeing to talk to her! Unable to hide her delight, she turned starry eyes on him.

'I'm grateful for your time, Leon.' Longingly she added, 'How is she?'

Hard eyes sliced into her delight, reminding her that she had a long way to go before she got what she wanted.

'Very well.'

She hesitated, needing to know more. 'Happy?' she asked lightly.

'I'm delirious, thank you,' he mocked, looking nothing of the sort.

Emma bit back her irritation. She'd be able to judge Lexi's state of mind soon enough. Leon might do everything in his power to restrict access, but surely no court would support him? A mother must count for something out here.

'I wondered,' she asked hesitantly, 'do you have any photos?'

The need in her voice was more than obvious. Let him know how much she cared, she thought, wondering why he didn't answer straight away. Leon ought to know how badly she wanted to see Lexi. He might then realise that the courts would recognise that too—and therefore be persuaded that Lexi's life would be enhanced by visits from her birth mother.

She held her breath when his hand slipped into the inner pocket of his jacket. Without a word he handed over a slim leather case. Emma's fingers shook as she slid the photos out and looked at her daughter for the first time in two long years.

'Oh!' she said breathily.

Still a sunny-faced child. Sturdy, laughing, obviously happy. In cute bathing costumes or sweet dresses, with her hair up in delightful bunches or dancing on her shoulders. On a boat, in a pool, surrounded by presents...

So many photos, she thought in wonder, blinking through her tears. Her heart somersaulted. Bleakly she realised that Leon must adore his niece. And...Lexi...would she adore him?

A pain scythed right through her. She fought back a moan. Perhaps she was making a mistake! Horrified, she raised her head to meet his devil-dark stare, her eyes huge with distress.

'Yes, Emma. She's happy. So why smash a child's care-free life?' he asked quietly.

She couldn't answer. A lump sat hard and hurting in her throat. She blinked at him in acute misery as her carefully constructed plans began to tumble down on her head.

John had insisted that Leon always spoke of Lexi as a chattel. Never with love. She knew that Leon had talked about doing his duty in looking after Lexi, and honouring a promise he'd made to his father.

Based on the fact that he'd told her he'd never wanted to assume responsibility for his niece, Emma had assumed that his interest in Lexi was minimal. Naturally she'd believed that Leon's own child must be the favourite and that little Lexi came a very poor second-best.

Whereas the opposite seemed to be true. Leon apparently kept the contents of a photo album on him, every picture depicting Lexi. Her mouth trembled and she touched her in-jured breast with a faltering hand. Briefly a flash of some-thing indefinable flickered in Leon's eyes. A glint of... triumph?

'Go home,' he murmured softly. 'Save yourself grief. And Lexi. Think of her feelings if you suddenly appear on the scene. The upheaval, the shock...'

He sounded confident, utterly sure that she'd accept the wisdom of his words. She frowned, trying to iron out the discrepancy between John's report and the lovingly collected photographs kept close to Leon's heart.

John wouldn't lie—he had her own best interests at heart. Whereas Leon would do anything to dissuade her. So what was the truth of the matter? How could she be sure that she wasn't about to tear her daughter's life apart?

Her heart cramped. If she ever thought she'd damage Lexi, she'd abandon all plans of abduction. Maybe, she thought in dismay, her journey had been all for nothing!

CHAPTER TWO

EMMA struggled to unravel the truth. Leon couldn't be trusted. It would suit him very well if she gave up and went home, abandoning her child for ever.

She frowned. Something was nagging at the back of her mind. To do with the photos. What could it be? There were a lot. And... Her head lifted as it dawned on her what was wrong. Lexi had been alone in every shot.

'Is she in any other photos you've got? Could you have a look?' she asked, pretending to be dispirited in the hope she'd catch Leon off guard.

'You've seen them all. These are the only ones I have on me.' He purred, sure it seemed, of success.

'Just the ones of Lexi.'

'My beloved niece,' he said with surprisingly believable sincerity, piling on the sentiment.

She could have hit him. That confirmed her theory! Every knotted up muscle in her body relaxed and she stared at him with cold blue eyes.

'How extraordinary! It's a strange father who carries a dozen or so snaps of his niece but none of his own child.' She gave him a sugary smile, seeing that he looked totally disconcerted. Her eyes gleamed. 'Might there be a reason for that?' she murmured.

'What reason could there be?' He growled, an extraordinary tautness bringing his cheekbones into high relief.

'Deception,' she retorted, lashing him with a scathing glance. 'I think that you knew I'd be here and so you deliberately collected the photos to show me—'

'A kind gesture, surely?' He frowned at her.

'Not under the circumstances, no.' she replied, lifting a

36

challenging chin. 'You've made it clear that you don't want me to meet my daughter. Why, then, would you whet my appetite by showing photos of her? To tease me? I think not. You wouldn't risk increasing my desire to see her.'

His eyes blackened. 'How about pride?' he said bitingly. 'To show you how well she is cared for—'

'You don't fool me!' she scoffed. 'John's told me about your indifference to Lexi—'

'Has he, now?' Leon muttered grimly. 'Has he indeed?'

'Yes. And it broke my heart to know she wasn't important to you.'

'She is—'

'Oh, maybe as a Kyriakis, as your brother's child, but not because you feel any love for her. I got the impression she was a nuisance. My *daughter*! That's what's hurt me so much. She's with you because of your wretched pride and because you think you're better than me—'

'That last part is certainly true.'

'We'll see about that!' she said flaring, beside herself with anger. 'Lexi needs me. I'm here to bring some love into my daughter's life.' She choked.

'You'll bring confusion and uncertainty—'

'No, I won't,' she insisted hotly. 'I can't believe you almost succeeded in deterring me. How could I have been so stupid as to doubt my own instincts? You cynically assembled those photos to imply that Lexi is the most important person in your life—'

'She is!' Leon declared furiously, his hands balling into tight fists.

'Pull the other one!' she scorned. Her head was up, her hair flying about her face as she shook with indescribable anger. 'Common sense says that your wife and your own daughter must be dearer to you. You may well flinch. I've sussed you out, haven't I? You're *despicable*, Leon, attempting to prevent her from seeing the one person who can give her real love. I know you begrudge looking after her—and

I'm going to prove it. I can't *believe* you staged this farcical show of devotion!'

'You're wrong about my feelings for Lexi,' he said, his voice vibrating with passion. His eyes glittered. 'And I would warn you to be wary of what Sefton says. He has ulterior motives—'

'Yes. He *cares*!'

'But who for? Just consider carefully everything he says,' Leon said shortly.

'He told me you were sly,' she shot. 'I think that's pretty accurate. Meeting me here *wasn't* a coincidence, was it? I suppose the immigration officer tipped you off so I had to sit about cooling my heels while you ransacked your house for photos of my child.'

'Staphos called me, yes,' he conceded. 'We're fishing buddies. He had a hunch you must be Taki's widow. But I always carry these photos.' He contemplated her thoughtfully. 'I wasn't expecting to see you for another couple of years.' A sardonic curl deepened the etched arches of his mouth. 'Are you on the run?'

She glared. 'Of course not. I was released six months ago.'

'Six months!' he exclaimed with exaggerated surprise. 'And you were so desperate to see your beloved daughter that you dawdled straight here!'

'I've been ill.' She flung the words at him, seething at the injustice of his remark. 'That's why my sentence was reduced.'

'You've recovered remarkably well,' he observed with heavy sarcasm.

'Good nutrition, a healthy lifestyle and a clear conscience!'

'I can believe two out of three,' he mocked.

She couldn't fence with him any more. She felt emotionally drained. Anger and anxiety weren't good for her and she tried to avoid it. Unfortunately there was something about Leon that made her blood boil. Whatever had happened to her self-control? she wondered gloomily. One snarl from Leon and it ran away with its tail between its legs.

'This isn't getting us anywhere,' she said wearily. 'We must come to some arrangement. And I'd rather we talked where I can sit down out of the sun. I'm not fully fit and this heat saps my strength.' Longingly she thought of a long drink in a frosted glass with ice in it. 'Perhaps we can find a taverna.'

Leon shrugged and picked up her case. 'My car's over there. If you insist on wasting your time...'

'Being reunited with my child is hardly a waste of time,' she rebuked icily.

She trudged behind Leon feeling as battered as if she'd gone twenty rounds in a boxing ring. Maybe she'd beaten him in the first battle of wits, but there would be more difficulties put in her way and she must rally her energies and be on full alert.

'Staying long?' He flung the words curtly over his shoulder.

She hurried to catch up, conscious that every taxi driver was watching their progress with interest. Tired of hedging, she decided to be frank.

'As long as it takes.'

He glanced down at her defiant face, his mouth creaking up in a faintly mocking smile.

'Then we'd better find you a home you can grow old and grey in.'

With a groan, Emma slapped her hand to her forehead in dismay. 'I forgot. I've got one. A home, I mean.'

'Where?' he enquired quickly.

She frowned. 'That's the trouble—I don't know. I should have got the address from John before he left. He's found me some cheap rooms to rent in the town.'

'He usually stays at the Hotel Zantos,' Leon commented drily. 'Five star. Two pools. Sauna—'

Emma hardly heard. She was concentrating on staying upright. She'd taken on too much, she realised gloomily. She wasn't fit enough yet for all this hassle. She was dead on her feet and had nowhere to go for a good bath and an extended collapse.

'I've got to call him,' she said wearily. She closed her eyes and gave a heavy sigh. 'Do you have a phone?' she asked in a small voice. 'Please, Leon,' she whispered, on the edge of exhaustion.

He studied her uplifted face, tension stretching the skin over his taut jaw.

'Let's get across the road to the shade of the trees,' he said quietly, as taxis, hire-cars and coaches roared into life, heralding the arrival of another planeload of tourists.

Too feeble, too close to tears to reply, she allowed his proprietorial hand to descend on the small of her back while he shepherded her through the mêlée. His palm burned its imprint into her flesh and when she stumbled in confusion his arm slipped more securely around her waist.

Its instant comfort baffled her even more. He was her adversary and she should cringe from his touch. But then, it had been a long time since a man had held her close, years since she'd felt safe and protected.

Her eyes grew huge. That last occasion had been when she and Leon had been together. He'd kissed her goodbye the night before his engagement to Marina. She remembered it well. Lingering. Loving.

She winced. The wonderful strength and pressure of Leon's arm was a false security. He'd have thrown her to the lions if he could have found some lurking near the hire-cars.

'All right?' he asked quietly when they reached the other side.

His head was bent to hers in query. The soft hairs on her cheek tingled from the drift of his breath. Something warm and disturbing was coiling in her stomach and sharpening her senses even while weakening her body. And then he had dropped the case and was turning her to him with a surprising gentleness.

Without any effort on her part, her eyes closed in response. His breath came warm and quick on her sensitised mouth. She felt like putty in his hands, too tired to fight his hypnotic appeal. It was both wonderful and frightening. She had to get away. Fast.

She opened her eyes a fraction. 'I...I don't feel too good,' she whispered miserably, her heart sinking as she realised that she was too fatigued to successfully plead her case for access.

'In that case, let's forget the taverna and cheap digs and get an upgrade,' he murmured soothingly.

'I just want John,' she said in panic. And to sleep for a hundred years... Her eyes met his and were misted with longing.

'Touching. But you can make do with me.' Tight-lipped again, Leon pushed her resisting body into the car. 'Relax. You'll snap tendons, screwed up like that. What are you worried about? As sure as hell I'm not in a mood for abduction.'

'Once was enough, was it?' she flashed, obstinately remaining stiff as a board in the seat.

'More than.'

Simmering darkly, he leaned across, intent on fastening the seat belt for her. Emma swallowed as first his beautifully smooth golden jaw and then the ever-kissable nape of his neck came to within a hair's breadth of her breathless mouth. Incapable of stopping herself, she inhaled, her senses reeling from the clean, fresh maleness of him.

And she was too weak to protest, too shattered by the journey and, perhaps, the emotional excitement, to prevent him from invading her space and protesting that she was perfectly capable of fastening her own seat belt. Because she wasn't.

Unaccountably panic-stricken, she stared out of the window. It was the upsurge of memories, she thought. Her brain was playing tricks with her body, reminding her of love and tenderness…

Her eyes widened as she saw that her case had been abandoned some distance away. 'My case! It'll be stolen!' she cried in agitation.

He paused, turning to look at her. This close, his eyes seemed as black as newly hacked coal. Suddenly Emma couldn't get her breath, and sat stunned by the impact of the electrical charge that leapt across the gap between them both and which wrenched fiercely at her pained heart.

The man was married. He ought to keep himself switched in neutral, she thought crossly.

'Your case is safe. We're *honest* on this island,' he snapped.

She winced as his words seemed to slide like a cruel knife into her ribs. The seat belt finally slotted into place. Leon moved back with a tantalising waft of lemony soap and a blur of glossy dark hair and polished skin. His hair still curled defiantly at the nape, she saw, remembering his efforts to keep it strictly in check.

Her door slammed. She watched him retrieve the case and stride back, grim-faced. For a moment or two she could breathe again. It was a long time since she'd felt so limp and short of oxygen. Presumably anxiety and the heat had affected her.

Emma groaned. This was bad news. Over the next few days she *must* be able to cope with whatever Leon threw at her. The way things were going, she could well have a court case to cope with.

After that, if she eventually won access, she'd need to be at her physical peak if she was to respond to Lexi's needs.

Emma let out a deep sigh. She'd intended to hire a car and take her daughter to the beach. There they could make sandcastles, play in the water and generally have a good time.

However long it took, she meant to forge a strong and loving relationship with Lexi. She knew she could do that.

Her love for her child had survived despite the long separation. Her illness had intensified the knowledge that only one thing in the world mattered: being with her emotion-starved daughter and showing her what it was like to be truly loved.

She leaned back, worried. There was so much to do before Lexi was safe in England. There would be the hazardous journey with Lexi and John: boat-hopping up the chain of Ionian Islands, a secret landing on the Greek coast and then the long drive across Europe.

Throughout the trip she'd have to be focussed exclusively on Lexi, playing games to pass the time, keeping her amused and happy so that it all seemed great fun.

It had sounded perfectly feasible back in England. The route had been mapped, John had returned from his recce with an optimistic report on secluded coves and rarely used roads. But... She bit her lip. If she wasn't strong enough—if she fell ill...

Horribly daunted by what lay ahead, she passed a shaking hand over her forehead as Leon slid into the driver's seat. Doubts multiplied. If she lacked energy she'd never cope. Lexi would feel abandoned and bewildered.

Her breath caught in a choking anguish in her throat. The thought of failure made her feel sick.

'You look shot to pieces. I think you need cheap digs like a hole in the head,' he commented shrewdly, starting up the car.

'A luxury hotel would be preferable, but beyond my funds,' she retorted, wallowing crossly in the ambitious thought of a soft bed, room service and an *en suite* bathroom.

'Wait and see what I can come up with,' he said, sounding smug. 'If you don't like where I take you, we'll ring your lawyer and get you to his rat-infested hovel instead.'

'Promise,' she mumbled, almost past caring about rats as long as there was a mattress to rest her weary body.

She let out a long and whispering sigh and felt his dark glance on her parted lips.

'On my father's head,' he said softly. 'Take a break for now,' he added, as if soothing a fractious child. 'Sleep. I'll wake you when we arrive.'

Emma did her best to disobey but felt her heavy lids closing like shutters. Yet Leon's image stayed to torment her remorselessly: the classic Greek profile, thick lashes concealing liquid black eyes, patrician nose and achingly sensual mouth. Before getting into the car he'd removed his jacket, his open-necked cream shirt moulding to his muscular back and torso.

Her breath quickened. He was dangerously attractive. Tension hung in the air so thickly she could feel it. Even from a short distance away his magnetism poured over her like a relentless tide till she felt she might drown beneath it.

But why was he being considerate? It would amuse him to see her living in the hovel he'd so mockingly described. She racked her brains to determine why he was going out of his way to find her decent accommodation. And could only come up with one answer. For some reason, as yet unknown to her, it suited him.

And therefore his offer should be rejected. Hovel it was, then, she thought glumly.

Music filtered drowsily into her subconscious. Gentle zithers, a haunting refrain. She felt herself relaxing and began to surrender to desperately needed sleep.

Lexi was close, she thought dreamily. Almost in her arms. Another huge sigh of pleasure was expelled from her soft lips and, although she slept, her hands unconsciously sought refuge at her wounded left breast.

Leon shook his head to clear it. He'd be fine if he kept remembering that there was vengeance in her soul. She'd do anything to hurt him. And Lexi was the weapon she'd choose.

He knew he couldn't keep mother and daughter apart. Eventually the court would be faced with Emma's doting mother act and grant access. His only hope was if he could convince them she was not a reformed character.

He glanced at her then scowled at the road ahead, trying to eradicate the sight of her lush breasts swelling beneath her dress. He ached from wanting her. But that was out of the question.

He dragged his mind back to the problem. Emma would visit Lexi and one day make an abduction attempt. He thought of the vulnerable little Lexi being hauled across Europe with two strangers and his chest expanded with uncontainable rage. Sefton was a creep. He didn't trust him an inch.

He had to keep Emma away. And to do that, he needed clear evidence that she wasn't fit to go near his niece and that any contact would be harmful.

His pulses quickened. An idea was forming in his mind. One that would kill two birds with one stone.

He too had a weapon. Sex.

CHAPTER THREE

'IT'S lovely,' Emma said longingly, wandering around the villa's elegant sitting area in awe. Quality floor tiles. Stunning traditional furniture, heavily carved, the sofas invitingly squishy and with huge cushions she could picture herself sinking into... She groaned. Heaven. 'But I can't possibly stay...'

'Let me make you some tea,' called Leon from the kitchen area beyond. 'Then I'll explain the set-up.'

'Tea!' She sighed, instantly seduced by the sound of a kettle being filled. 'OK. Then I must call John,' she insisted, being ruthless with herself. And very annoyed by the wistful note that had crept into her voice.

She paused, even more irritated to be disconcerted by the breadth of Leon's tautly muscled back as he stretched up to one of the blue-painted units. It was a back. Gorgeous, granted, but nothing to quiver about.

'I expect there's some chocolate cake somewhere,' he mused, bending to search in one of the lower cupboards.

In doing so he provided her with an unwanted but riveting view of his neat and muscular rear beneath the straining material of his linen trousers. She primmed her mouth in exasperation.

His body had been spectacular. Still was. She really must get out more. Appalled at her rampaging pulses, she did an about turn and concentrated on her suspicions.

'Just where and what is this place? I doubt I can afford it,' she remarked coolly, parking herself at the stylish marble dining table adorned with blue china pots of all shapes and sizes. She picked one up. It was Chinese. 'Leon!' she cried,

46

breathless with hope and abandoning her assumed indifference. 'Is this your house?'

He glanced amiably at her, the dazzle of his beautiful smile raising her blood pressure a few notches. She glared it back down again where it belonged.

'It's mine,' he replied. 'But not where I live.'

What did that mean? she wondered, while he put a temptingly rich dark cake and two plates on the table in front of her. He seemed very much at home, very familiar with the place.

Leon pulled out one of the wrought iron chairs opposite her and sat down on the comfortable linen cushion, his muscular arms resting on the table. Emma dragged her fascinated gaze away from their tanned strength and obliterated all thought of being held by those arms.

But her treacherous body had remembered the fluttering of her heart when he'd escorted her across the road earlier, and the almost intimate pressure of his firm hand. And so she found her voice stupidly husky when she asked what had just occurred to her.

'I hope this isn't a secret hideaway for your mistress?'

His eyes glowed. 'My...mistress?' he said slowly.

It was crazy, but she had the distinct impression that he was thinking of her in that role. Perhaps he remembered how good they'd been... Her breath rasped in, every bone and sinew in her body back in memory lane. Blue eyes locked with brown. He was remembering too, she realised in panic, shaken by his blatant hunger.

'Leon!' she said croakingly and furiously cleared her throat. 'I don't know why you've brought me here, but if it's to...to...'

'To what?' He smiled beguilingly. 'Why don't you indulge?'

She blinked, eyes wide and alarmed. 'In...what?'

'Cake,' he said, purring, with the charming, lopsided smile

which had weakened her knees on countless occasions before. 'What did you imagine I meant?'

She blushed. But she wasn't mistaken. She knew desire when she saw it. Knowing Leon's arrogant assumption that all women would come running if he snapped his fingers, knowing how little he respected her in particular, she was sure he was expecting her to say, Yes, please, and, Thank you, when he made a move on her.

He probably assumed that because she'd been deprived of male company for some time, she was up for grabs. And, she remembered grimly, he'd used her purely for sexual pleasure before.

'I'm not hungry,' she said haughtily. He could make of that what he liked.

'I am.'

She flashed a sharp glance at him. His teeth were biting into the chocolate cake, but his tone had been laden with throaty sexuality. That was why she was here, then. For a bit of slap and tickle.

Misery washed over her, far out of proportion to her disappointment in his motives. For a brief moment she had thought that he was being nice to her in finding somewhere for her to stay. But he did want to use her again. She felt like crying.

'You eat away, then,' she said. 'While I call John. Where's the phone?'

His hand caught her arm in a gentle but inescapable grip. 'Hold on a moment. You can't turn down a chance like this. You want somewhere to stay, don't you?'

She shivered. Something hot and fierce ricocheted between them, ripping through her tense body and cutting her legs from beneath her. Incapable of staying on her feet, she collapsed into the chair again. But, as she did so, his fingers slithered up the softness of her arm.

Before she could stop herself, she let out a gasp. The sensation had been electrifying, every cell in her body responding as if they had been individually charged. Appalled, she wrenched herself free, her mouth tight with disapproval. She knew his game. And would resist.

'Not with strings attached. I'll take the hovel and its rats rather than your love nest and you.'

'This has never been a love nest,' he said, his voice soft and low. It vibrated deeply into her fractured nerves, soothing them. And alarming her even more. 'It's just one of four villas I've had built for the holiday trade. Diversification.'

She wasn't convinced. Too much valuable china. Sensationally beautiful drapes at the windows. Kitchen equipment to die for. Terracotta busts in niches. Murano glass lampshades and hand-carved furniture. Holiday trade!

'Luxury market, presumably?' she scorned in disbelief.

'Of course.'

'So where are the occupants? The designer-label buckets and spades?'

'It's not quite finished and nobody's used it yet,' he explained, his mouth quirking up in amusement.

'Except for whoever's partial to tea and chocolate cake,' she muttered.

'My...designer used this as a base.'

'Ah. I understand. Female, blonde and beautiful?' she asked sourly before she could stop herself.

His eyes seemed to bore into her skull. 'The description fits her.' He smiled faintly. 'Does that bother you, Emma?'

'It ought to bother your wife,' she pointed out, hating herself for minding. He was dangerous. A womaniser with an overactive sex drive. And, she thought indignantly, her daughter was in his care!

'Ex-wife,' he corrected softly.

Her eyes widened in astonishment. 'Oh. I didn't know...' Emma tried to interpret his expression but it was unreadable. She remembered only too vividly how her own marriage had disintegrated, leaving scars and recriminations behind. And now…yes, there was a hint of pain in his eyes. Her face softened in sympathy. 'I am sorry, Leon. It's—'

'I don't want to talk about it.'

'No. Of course not…'

Extraordinarily, Emma wanted to comfort him. He seemed…tense, perhaps caught up in his own grief.

'Stay,' he urged.

She didn't dare. He was fancy-free and twice as dangerous. Loathe to drag herself out again, she raised her hands in a helpless gesture.

'I can't let John down. He's gone to all that trouble—'

'Not *very* much trouble, I imagine,' Leon said cynically.

'I said I'd phone him—'

'But this is so much more convenient than somewhere in town, twenty minutes away,' he argued. And temptingly he added, 'We're actually on my land, Emma. My house is the other side of the olive grove.'

Her eyes rounded in a wildly revived hope. What was he implying? He wouldn't let her come this close to his house if he didn't intend to let her see Lexi, would he? Or was this a cruel joke, to tease her with, before letting her down—the so-near-and-yet-so-far trick?

'It sounds too perfect. Why bring me here?' she asked suspiciously.

'Simple.' He threw her one of his devastating smiles. 'I thought that if you're to be on the island then you might as well be somewhere I can keep an eye on you.'

She glared. 'I'm to be spied on!'

He shrugged. 'You're not doing anything you shouldn't, are you?' He waited for her to comment but she just stared doggedly, refusing to be drawn. She watched him dig deep into his range of smiles and select one that was utterly persuasive and suspiciously benign. 'It's rent-free and near your daughter,' he informed her. 'Can you afford to turn my offer down?'

'Depends who I share with,' she said warily, very much tempted.

'No one. Other than whoever you invite.' He reached across the table, his fingers almost touching hers. But not quite. She looked at them, dazed, every nerve in her body tingling as she waited for his hand to inch a little closer. 'You'd like to be close to Lexi, wouldn't you?' he coaxed.

Brute! She stared helplessly, her heart lurching as she imagined little tea parties with Lexi here... A walk to the nearby village—if there was one—for ice creams...

'Yes...' She choked. How could she trust him? 'But—'

'I'll make the tea while you think about it,' he said with warm understanding.

Too warm. He was up to something. 'I've thought. I don't want to be spied on,' she said reluctantly, common sense overruling her yearning heart.

He brought over a blue and white teapot and pulled his chair even closer to hers, studying her with an expression of concern.

'But, Emma, you're tired. You don't feel well.' His voice did its stroking act on her, evoking a dangerous need for sympathy and a shoulder to lean on. 'Surely,' he murmured, 'you don't want to go charging across the countryside to find Sefton's nasty little rented room?'

No. She didn't. But she'd have to. The thought of it made her feel weak. 'So you're Sir Galahad now, are you?' she muttered.

He gave a small chuckle that made him seem eminently harmless and friendly. But she knew better.

'Hardly. But see it from my point of view. Supposing you're taken ill in some backstreet dump in Zante town? How would that look? There'd be a scandal when it gets out what our relationship is.'

'Oh. Your precious reputation!' she snapped waspishly.

'Absolutely.' He leaned forwards earnest-faced, apparently unaware of her sarcasm. 'It would be unforgivable if I did not offer hospitality to my late brother's wife, whatever I think of her, whatever she has done.'

Thoughtfully she picked up a slice of cake. 'That makes sense,' she remarked, nibbling off the layer of chocolate icing reflectively. She saw him smiling to see her eating despite her declaration that she wasn't hungry. And went for the kill. 'You can't afford to have the courts thinking you're vindictive.'

'Courts?' he asked, raising his brows. His smile was pure charm as he turned her gibe back on her. 'I hope we can come to an arrangement without their involvement.'

Her heart thudded with excitement. But she kept her head. 'You were worried about Lexi's welfare earlier on,' she declared. 'What's changed your mind?'

He raised expressive shoulders and poured out the tea. 'You. I did everything I could to dissuade you but obviously you're determined to see her, come hell or high water. I can't stop you. You *are* her mother. If I forbid you to see her and you put in a complaint then tongues would wag—'

'Bad for your reputation,' she suggested, seeing that this could work in her favour.

'My honour would be tarnished. No one would understand that my motives were purely in Lexi's interests. I don't like this, Emma. But providing we go about this sensitively, I don't see how I can decently refuse.'

Her eyes shone as his words sank into her tired brain. 'Oh, *Leon*!' she gasped, overwhelmed.

He pushed the crumbs around his plate with his forefinger. 'Don't imagine you're having things all your own way. Having conceded the *possibility* of access, I want to hammer out the when and how and what with *you*—and not some lawyer.' His voice lowered. 'She's too important to be stuck in the middle of an unpleasant legal tussle. And I prefer to have some say in what happens to her. So we do this on my terms. Understood?'

Emma stared. She could hardly believe that he was actually acknowledging her rights at last. And if they could do this amicably then it would save time—and thousands of pounds in fees. She would be spending time with Lexi—with Leon's blessing—and her daughter would be back in England sooner than she'd ever imagined.

Her smile grew in magnitude till it irradiated her face. 'Thank you,' she said breathily. 'I agree. I don't want her upset either. I just want to see her, Leon.'

'So you'll stay here in this villa,' he said quietly.

'Yes! Yes!'

She was crying and laughing. He didn't know what to do. She sat there, tears trickling down her cheeks, obviously trying to control herself. And failing. The point of her tongue slid out to capture each silvery droplet and Leon felt an extraordinary lurch of sentiment and compassion before he realised these were probably tears of exhaustion.

And that he could use this moment to his advantage.

He felt a brief sense of distaste but something else—perhaps sympathy, perhaps desire—drove him to push back his chair and bend over her.

He'd had to concede more than he'd wanted. But she was on his land, under his eyes, subject to his demands. It could have been worse. Under Sefton's guidance, she would have gone to the courts and perhaps won unsupervised access. She might have told Lexi immediately who she was. And that wasn't in his plan at all.

Gently he wiped her eyes, steeling himself to ignore her startled look and the appealing flutter of her wet lashes. With great care he dabbed at her face and leaned close to wipe her mouth.

It took great self-control not to kiss her. It was too soon.

'Now we've got that out of the way, why don't you drink your tea and I'll show you around?' he suggested, far too huskily for his liking. He mustn't frighten her away.

'Oh, Leon!' she said breathily, almost ruining his plan by

turning starry eyes on him. 'I'm so glad we're not at daggers drawn any longer!'

He had to move away. And hide his shamed face. He hated this but he didn't see any other way. Deception wasn't in his nature and it went against everything he stood for. But he'd do this for Lexi. She had to be protected from Emma.

'Come and see the view. It's worth staying for alone,' he said, managing to sound hearty, and he flung open the back door.

'Oh-h-h!'

Tears forgotten, Emma jumped up, enchanted. Framed by the doorway was a sunken terrace surrounding a swimming pool, its water an invitingly clear aquamarine. Flowers tumbled in profusion from Ali Baba pots around it and already she could smell the scented breeze that ruffled the leaves of the orange and lemon trees shading one end of the terrace.

Stretching across the skyline she could see a range of green undulating hills. And from their wooded slopes, to the citrus orchard beyond the pool lay a fertile valley filled with silvery olives and vines and the tall, pencil-slim shapes of dark cypress trees. One lone and magnificent cypress had been planted strategically by the pool, and it soared like a malachite rocket into the bright blue sky.

'You like?' Leon enquired close by.

She'd drifted to the doorway to gape without knowing it. The view was affecting her strangely. She felt calm and at peace, almost as if she was responding emotionally to the timeless beauty of the landscape. Perhaps because she was so keyed up.

But it *was* stunning. She could spend hours drinking it in, smelling the scents on the warm breeze, feeling the sun on her tired body.

'I like,' she murmured with quiet fervour, her eyes dreamy.

'You can swim any time, night or day. It's quite private,' Leon said.

She saw herself in the turquoise water, letting it ripple over her skin. Her eyes glazed, her thoughts racing. She'd buy one of those blow-up chairs for the pool. A ball. She could see herself and her daughter; laughing, splashing, cuddling...

'Does Lexi like the water?' she asked, suddenly horribly aware that she knew nothing about her child. Her nerves began to jangle. This wouldn't be easy...

'Swims like a fish. She'll love it here,' he assured her. 'Better than a hovel?'

She grinned. 'I'm sure John chose somewhere utterly charming and cosy,' she defended.

Leon took her elbow. 'Forget him. Come and explore. There's a ground-floor bedroom this way, with its own terrace and bathroom,' he said, guiding her through to the living room end.

'I'm not quite sure what's happened. You were so hostile when we met,' she mused, reluctant to believe in his conversion. 'I was somewhere to the left of Satan's auntie.'

He chuckled, smiling down at her and she wished he wouldn't. His hand slid casually up her arm and his fingers absently stroked her sensitised skin. It was all she could do not to let out a gasp but she kept it lodged in her chest, hard and hurting.

'I know. Can you blame me? I have to protect Lexi's interests.' He smiled again, less certainly, but the warmth in his eyes melted her doubts. 'But I realise now that I have no choice. For Lexi's sake we must try to be civil to one another.'

Emma released her breath and smiled back, deliriously happy. In these surroundings, away from Leon's interference, she could spend long hours with Lexi. Picnics. Reading stories. Learning about her child. She felt dizzy with excitement.

'When can I see her, Leon?' she asked eagerly.

'Bath, shower and so on through there, bedroom here...' he went on, urging her forward as if he hadn't heard. A light came on in the darkened room. 'What do you think?'

Spectacular. His designer had an enviable style. She couldn't believe her luck.

She glanced around the spacious bedroom with its cool tiles and beautifully carved four-poster. Leon had detached himself and was drawing back the two sets of fine lawn drapes—royal blue and a contrasting white to tone in with the colour scheme in the room. He lifted the latch of the full-length shutters and the room was instantly bright with sunshine.

'Terrace.' His arm swept out in an invitation.

Emma pushed aside the fluttering drapes and went out. She murmured something complimentary about the fabulous roses and persevered.

'I'd like to meet Lexi tomorrow,' she said firmly.

'Of course. Come upstairs.'

She was dumbfounded. Ecstatic! Had it really been that easy? 'Leon!' she cried in glee, hurrying after his retreating figure. 'Do you really mean that?'

At the top of the stairs he turned and she, lost in her world of dreams and delight, almost bumped into him.

'Whoa!' he said, amused.

His hands steadied her and the dancing light in his eyes clouded. Emma could feel the heavy pulses in his thumbs where they pressed into the soft flesh of her arms. She wilted beneath his silence, the intensity of his gaze liquefying her bones and driving all sense out of her head.

'Leon…'

She felt him quiver. His name had been but a whisper from her dry throat. The sexual tension held her as his captive, and she found her head tipping back so that her hair flowed down her back like ribbons of honey. A gesture of surrender.

Bewildered, she tried in vain to say something banal to hide her overwhelming desire to be kissed by those laughing, edible lips. But all she could do was to stare into his eyes, her mouth ready and her entire body waiting, hoping.

'I think,' he muttered brusquely, suddenly whisking away

and collecting her case, 'you're overtired. I'll put this in the downstairs bedroom for you and then I'll leave you in peace—'

'Yes,' she croaked hastily, horrified and shame-faced at her shocking reaction. She *was* tired. Emotionally muddled. That was it. Mortified, she realised that Leon must have interpreted the message in her eyes—in her explicit body language. And yet he'd rejected the chance to kiss her.

She stood in the middle of the room, scarlet to the roots of her hair. Clearly, she'd been wrong about him. Maybe he had flirted. Or perhaps he couldn't help projecting sex appeal. Or she'd wanted... Yes, she had to admit—shaming though it was—that she found him intensely attractive.

It was perfectly possible then that she'd read all the wrong things in the way he'd looked at her. It was the only explanation. Because when she'd let her hunger surface, he'd been horrified because he genuinely despised her.

Was that it? Her mind was so befuddled and tired she couldn't think straight. She had to explain...

He was already in the bedroom, slamming down her case. In a temper, it seemed—annoyed that he'd got himself trapped with a sex-starved wimp. She inhaled several times to calm herself. She'd almost made a disastrous mistake.

'I'm so exhausted I hardly know what I'm doing,' she called, her voice genuinely shaky.

'Thought so. You'll need food. I'll have some things delivered.'

Nerves jangling, she waited till he emerged, avoiding her eyes. Her brain was beginning to function again. He'd said he was leaving... She felt a stab of fear when she realised that she didn't know where she was.

'You...you haven't dumped me somewhere inaccessible?' she asked anxiously as he strode purposefully to the door and opened it. For all she knew, his house was miles away. And she had no transport. She was virtually a prisoner... 'Leon, don't leave me!' she began in panic.

His burning gaze flicked to meet hers. He said nothing, but he didn't have to. She knew shock when she saw it. Emma's hand flew to her mouth.

'I meant... I—meant...' she stammered incoherently.

'Later,' he said thickly. And marched out.

Later, she thought. Later...what? Had he said, See you later, and she'd missed the first part? He had mumbled.

She stood with her eyes closed, waiting for the waves of warmth to stop running in her veins and directing her leaping pulses to settle down. Foolishly she thought of him and instantly the sensations returned: the hammering heartbeat, the sense of reckless abandon, the terrible desire to melt into his arms.

The past was not done with. Because he'd left her so abruptly all those years ago, she had never really wiped him from her memory. Taki had accused her of that once, when she'd refused his drunken attentions.

'It's him!' he'd screamed, totally losing control. 'You think of him when we make love. You speak his name in your sleep!'

She'd been horrified. Because it was true—she *had* thought of Leon and his tender, passionate and sensitive lovemaking. It had been the only way to cope with Taki's rough and coarse approach. And her silence had fuelled Taki's anger.

He had taken her then, brutally stifling her cries with a crushing hand. But he'd never touched her again.

She shuddered. Her knowledge of men was minimal. Just the two brothers. One who'd taken her beyond herself, to the outermost reaches of pleasure. The other had kept her too close to harsh reality, the discomfort, the ugliness, the baseness of sex.

So, she mused, she had mistakenly put Leon and his ability to arouse her in a category he didn't deserve. All these years, despite her hatred of him, she'd thought of him as a great lover. And now she was face to face with him again, that myth was being perpetuated in her stupid brain.

Idiot. He couldn't be the only man in the world who took his time and was unselfish! It was just technique. Nothing more. And she *had* missed sex, and was very much in her prime, so all she had to do was to keep her distance from him and concentrate on Lexi.

She heaved a huge sigh and forced herself to begin unpacking. Halfway through, she realised she was shaking with fatigue, her strength sapped by the long and tension-filled day. Wearily she stripped off her clothes and showered, then closed the bedroom shutters to exclude the light. Fumbling in the darkness, she slid thankfully into bed.

Maybe she had no idea where she was on the island. But in a few hours she'd be seeing her child. She felt a lurch of apprehension in her chest and tried not to think about it yet. Her instincts would direct her.

Two years was a long time. So much had happened! In the warm darkness her fingers tentatively touched the deep scar on her breast, with its pinpoint tattoo marks which had guided the radiographer.

She'd been lucky. She might have died if the lump hadn't been discovered in time. And she was almost well again. The skin wasn't red there any more and the soreness had gone—the nausea too. Only the tiredness persisted and soon that would go too.

When the lump in her breast was diagnosed as malignant, she'd had just one reaction. Not fear for her own life, not regret or anger, but, *I want to see my child if I am to die*.

Well, she'd cheated death. In fact, she had a normal life-expectation. The future stretched ahead invitingly and she counted her blessings every single day. Every hour, she had vowed, would be lived to the full. She wouldn't waste the precious gift of life.

The thought of dying prematurely had stripped her world to the bone. Some things were important, most were trivial.

It didn't matter if it rained. She was there to see it, to feel and smell it. It didn't matter if a bus or a train was late. She was there to catch the next one.

But Lexi…she *was* important. Emma felt the passion fill her heart. She must have her child back, for both their sakes. Leon didn't care for anything other than his precious honour and reputation. Only she, Emma, would devote herself utterly to Lexi. Only she could truly love her child.

Leon would also realise that after a short while, she mused. He'd see her with Lexi and… Her heart thundered as her thoughts leapt ahead. Perhaps he'd even surrender Lexi willingly and she could forget the idea of abduction! The thought of going through with that terrified her now. But she would, if she had to.

Deeply happy, she conjured up the image of her daughter, now burned indelibly into her mind from the photographs she'd seen. Lexi was gorgeous. Emma's eyes glistened with tears. And she couldn't *wait* to see her in reality.

'Tomorrow, sweetheart!' she promised, as she curled up in the big, comfortable bed. 'The first day of our lives together.'

No more pain. No heartbreak. Just Lexi.

She'd never been happier. Everything she wanted lay within her grasp. Life was good again. Emma let out a deep, satisfied sigh. And let sleep enfold her.

CHAPTER FOUR

WHEN she woke it was a moment or two before she remembered where she was. By then she was aware of noises in the living room. She clutched the sheet to her chest, listening in alarm.

Leon had a key. The designer-blonde, presumably. Who else?

Wary of being surprised by a drug-crazed burglar whilst still stark naked, she slipped her feet to the floor and felt her way to where she'd left her clothes.

'Bother!' she said, yelping, when her fumbling hand knocked her small glass pill pots and her camera to the tiled floor.

'Emma? Are you all right?'

Leon, she registered in relief. But she couldn't find the pills. Didn't know if they'd spilled out... Worse, if anyone on the island stocked the unusual remedies...

'Emma,' bellowed the voice, right by the door.

'No, I'm not all right,' she yelled, still grovelling. At least it was only Leon. *Only!* 'Yes, I'm fine.' she cried, locating the tiny pots—intact. 'Don't come in,' she squealed in panic. 'Where's the light? Oh, darn it, where—?'

'I'm coming in!'

She heard the door handle turning. '*No!* I'm not *dressed*!'

There was a silence. The handle creaked back into place again and she grabbed the sheet, twisting it around her body securely before heading for the direction of the door. For a moment she hesitated then eased it open to find Leon apparently frozen to the spot on the other side.

'I knocked something over,' she explained with rather

61

breathless dignity, as his startled gaze flicked over her mummified figure. 'I couldn't find the light switch.'

He drew in a long, slow breath. 'Left of door.'

'Thanks.' She located it but decided to leave herself in relative shadow. She frowned, and broke the stiff silence. 'What exactly are you doing here?'

Leon seemed to be interested in the space just above her head. 'I brought your groceries. Supper. Breakfast.'

'Supper?' Startled, she looked at her watch. It was nine-thirty. Presumably, since the light was on in the living room, it was evening rather than morning. 'Oh. That's really kind of you, but...' This was awkward. Uncertain as to the etiquette of such a situation, she decided on a graceful retreat and a regrouping. 'Stay there. I'll be out in a minute.'

Closing the door she flicked on the light and hastily unwound the sheet. Supper. Was he staying? Her pulses began their remorseless tattoo and she gritted her teeth to outwit them. But she couldn't ignore her tingling, naked body and stomped to the wardrobe to find something to wear.

For some reason she was sorting through her clothes and tossing up between her only two decent outfits. A flirty red dress with a cleavage-displaying bodice and short skirt which she'd bought from a second-hand shop when she'd been several pounds thinner, and a green halter-neck top whose matching skirt slunk closely over her hips to the floor.

Or there was always a nice, safe shirt and jeans.

She smiled ruefully. Who was she kidding? She'd seen Leon. He'd been wearing a long-sleeved cream shirt with a toffee-coloured tie and beautifully cut trousers in a dark honey shade. With toning shoes.

Green, she decided impetuously, wriggling into the top. At least most of her was covered, except for her back which was hardly an erogenous zone.

She, too, could look groomed and expensive. She, too, was worthy to be a Kyriakis. Leon couldn't complain that she wasn't good enough for Lexi in this, she thought, reaching back to knot the ties securely.

'Sure you're OK?'

She flung up her tousled head. 'Yes. Coming.' And grabbed the skirt. Her fingers stilled as an awful realisation dawned. No bra—because of the low back. Mini briefs because of visible panty line. Help! How unwise could she be?

'I've put the potatoes on.'

'What?'

'Do you want aubergine salad or feta for starters?'

Starters? 'Aubergine,' she shouted. 'But—'

Her fingers dithered. She could wear the top with jeans— '*Stifado*, OK?'

Muttering under her breath, she hauled the skirt up and fastened its zip hastily. He was safe. He'd proved that earlier. She wanted to look her best. And she was starving.

'Depends what that is,' she said uncertainly, walking barefoot to where Leon stood, chopping and stirring.

'Beef. Red wine, garlic, onions, tomatoes and bay...'

He looked. And looked away fast, ruthlessly attacking the garlic innocently waiting for the pestle. Something had happened to his breathing system.

'Leon,' she said, unnervingly close. About two feet away, he reckoned. He'd have preferred twenty. Or the next village. 'I—I don't like to be difficult, but...I only eat organic food. It might sound cranky, but I don't want my body to deal with pesticides—'

'This is from my land,' he told her. 'It's completely organic, so there aren't any chemicals or pesticides and I don't think it's cranky at all. I think people should make up their own minds about what they eat. But it makes sense to play safe with children. I keep an eye on the things Lexi eats.'

She beamed, impressed and surprised. 'I'm really pleased. That means so much to me.' She surveyed his preparations. 'Leon, this is totally unexpected. You're being unnecessarily generous,' she said warmly.

He could see her bare arm out of the corner of his eye. It was smooth and golden and he wanted to touch it. Melt his mouth along it. Now.

The garlic suffered a ferocious pulverising.

'The main course was virtually cooked. My supper from home. You needed to eat and so did I. And we had to talk before you met up with Lexi.'

Frowning, he mixed the garlic with the lemon juice and herbs, wishing he could beat the hell out of it with a hand whisk and get rid of his tightly suppressed physical energy.

He'd thought he could handle this, that his desire to kiss her could be mastered. It was vital that it didn't look as if he was taking the initiative. But she was tearing into his self-control with every breath she took and every glance from those soft blue eyes.

She drifted somewhere behind him and the hairs rose on the back of his neck. And that wasn't all. He gritted his teeth, knowing he must get a grip of himself.

The seduction *must* seem to be her idea. Then he could go to the courts and block her attempts to see Lexi again, on the grounds that she was amoral. If he was going to huff and pant like an adolescent male over centrefolds then his plan wouldn't work.

'Leon.' She touched his arm and he jumped.

'What?'

'You *are* engrossed in the cooking.' She laughed, her face, her smile, her beautiful body right next to him. 'I said, who's looking after Lexi?'

He moved away and slammed a pan on for the rice. 'Marina.'

'Your ex-wife.' There was a chilly pause. 'You're on friendly terms with her, then?' she asked, but it was clear from her dubious tone that she didn't like the arrangement.

What did he tell her? At least, he thought ruefully, the mere mention of Marina had sent his hormones into hiding.

He felt able to face the green goddess without revealing his intentions.

'We still live together in the same house.'

'Good grief!' she cried, not unnaturally stunned.

'It's a large house.'

'Are you together for the sake of your daughter?' she asked, her eyes still wide with surprise.

'Yes,' he said in a low tone. 'For Soula's sake.'

Emma absorbed this for a moment. 'And how does Lexi fit into this?'

She was beautiful. No make-up but perfect skin, tousled hair straight from bed, making him think—

'Oh, dear. What's wrong?' she asked anxiously, noting his eyes were fixed intently upon her.

'Your hair. Not wrong...' His voice petered out.

She had raised her hands to her sexily tumbling waves, the action lifting her breasts to high, hard-tipped globes beneath the clinging material. She was near-naked, he thought, his throat drying.

'Bother. Sort of ruins my attempt at looking half decent. You mentioned food and out I rushed without brushing my hair.' She sighed. 'Tells you my priorities. I'll go and—'

'Don't. Leave it. It's only me,' he muttered, turning abruptly to weigh the rice.

His hands were shaking so much that he spilt half of it all over the tiled floor. Laughing, Emma searched the cupboards for a dustpan and he found himself having to cope with the sight of her slim, curvy rear outlined far too temptingly for any man to resist.

But he did his best to keep his hands to himself. What, however, was *she* doing? Seducing *him?* The dress... Her smiles... He sawed in a harsh breath. This was perfect.

He stared at the rice and couldn't remember if he'd weighed it or not. So he started all over again. Perhaps they'd be making love very soon, he thought, and was startled by his elation.

Emma was glad to be scrabbling on the floor. Leon seemed distracted. Almost curt. Perhaps he thought she'd jump him. Better put his mind at rest. And there was nothing better, she decided, than to talk about another man in warm and glowing terms.

'John's a good cook,' she offered, standing up flushed from her exertions.

A dark look. 'Oh, yes?'

'He makes the definitive spag. bol.,' she said with feeling, remembering how delicious it had been.

'I imagine a few Italians might disagree with you.'

Emma giggled at his dry comment. Then she continued with her paeans of praise, to make Leon think that she had a particular interest in John.

'I rate him very highly,' she said with genuine fondness and a faraway look in her eyes. He had been wonderful. Her rock. 'Not many lawyers would be so dedicated to their clients. I think I told you that I owe my freedom to him.'

Leon snorted. She was losing him, his attention directed to preparing the meal. Providing supper was evidently an attempt to meet her halfway, but his heart wasn't in it. That was understandable, she thought. He didn't want Lexi to be hurt.

Well, she'd have to coax him round. Make him see that she wasn't a monster but sensitive and caring. She'd pull out all the stops. That should do it.

She tipped the rice into the bin and washed her hands. 'Anything I can do to help?' she asked amiably.

'It's all done. Meat's heating up. Waiting for the rice and potatoes.'

'Then,' she said eagerly, grabbing an opened bottle of red wine and a couple of glasses, 'let's sit down and talk strategy.'

He seemed reluctant but after checking the oven he joined her and grudgingly accepted the glass of wine. Worried about the rigidity of his muscles, she decided to loosen him up a little and kicked off by curling up on the settee.

'Cheers,' she said merrily, hoping he'd be softened by her winning smile.

'Giamas.' He raised his glass, drank, and put it on the table beside him.

His mouth was moist with wine. She realised she was the one who was softening. 'Yammas,' she repeated throatily.

He looked at her, his eyes dark and glowing. She drew in a shuddery little breath, shaken by the bolt of heat which had hurled itself at her defenceless body.

Her wineglass slipped from her numb fingers and like lightning Leon sprang forward to save it, his left hand splaying out to shield her dress from splashes as he caught the glass in mid-air. Sitting in a state of paralysis, she could feel the heel of his hand pressing into the upper swell of her breast, burning, *burning*.

He didn't move a muscle. She stared at him, her eyes huge with confusion and he stared back. It was as if she were drugged, her lashes lowering drowsily, lips parting as she gasped for snatches of air. It was happening again, she thought helplessly, and could do nothing to stop it.

Their mouths were inches apart. She could feel the very heat of his body, was breathing his breath, being drawn by his magnetism closer, closer...

His hand lifted its pressure from her breast. It seemed he tore his gaze from hers. She blinked, high spots of colour reddening her cheekbones as he put her glass next to his and used his clean handkerchief to dab at the few splashes of wine on her bare shoulder.

'Woops,' she said in a feeble croak.

Leon slanted her a sideways glance and her pulses went haywire again. 'It was water last time,' he said huskily.

'Nerves.' She'd said too much.

Balanced on his haunches, far too near for her sanity, he

wiped the wine droplets from his own hand and studied her for a paralysing second or two.

'Why would you be nervous, Emma?'

She swallowed. Because something crazy was going on. A madness had possessed her. And she didn't like it, didn't want it, was terrified...

He put a tentative hand on hers. 'About Lexi?' he suggested softly.

'Yes,' she said squeakily.

That too. She lifted agonised eyes to his.

'I'll check the rice.'

He rose, taking her glass and his magnetism with him. Emma allowed herself a sigh of relief and tried to understand what and why she couldn't master her feelings, why she felt hopelessly drawn to him. Drawn! It was more like tumbling headlong into a warm and silky sea and allowing it to blot out the past, the present and future and not even caring.

She passed a shaking hand over her face.

'Here's a clean glass,' he murmured.

Her mouth stretched into a parody of a smile and she took it with great care. The wine hit her stomach quickly and revived her.

'I'm a renowned "dropper",' she told him brightly, as he strode back to the kitchen area.

'Remind me to provide plastic beakers when you come visiting,' he drawled. 'The *melijanosalata's* ready. Come and eat.'

Hugging that word 'visiting' to herself, Emma unwound her legs and slid them to the floor, quickly tugging her dress down where it had become rucked up. It didn't matter. Leon hadn't noticed. He was trying to light the candelabra on the table, the flickering light intensifying the planes and hollows of his face. His beauty made her stomach contract.

'It all looks wonderful,' she said huskily, glad to get her weakening body into a chair again.

'My pleasure. Enjoy.'

Her fork carried a neat stack of the aubergine salad to her mouth and she widened her eyes in surprise when she tasted it. 'Mmm! Gorgeous! I—' Her voice wavered. It seemed impossible for her to meet his eyes and not drown. 'Thanks for the food,' she babbled. 'For the gesture. For this. You must let me know what I owe you—'

Leon's eyes flickered. 'On the house.' He smiled, his eyes crinkling in the appealing way that had always sent her heart lurching. 'I need your co-operation, you see.'

She might have known. She hid her peculiar disappointment by eating. 'Go on,' she mumbled warily, between mouthfuls.

He took a deep breath. 'There is a slight problem about you seeing Lexi.'

She felt immediately sick. 'No,' she whispered.

'Please, Emma,' he said earnestly, 'it's nothing insurmountable. The trouble is, that Lexi knows nothing about you.'

'Oh. Is that all? Well, you can fill her in, and so can I. I've got a picture of me somewhere, I brought it specially—'

'No.' There was something about his manner that made her clutch at her throat. 'I mean,' he said quietly, 'that she doesn't know you even exist.'

She gave a horrified gasp. '*Leon!* How could you do this to her? To me?'

'What was I to say? That her mother was away? She has no concept of time—I couldn't tell her that you'd turn up in a few years. Besides,' he admitted, 'I hoped you wouldn't.'

'She would have asked about me at some stage,' Emma cried.

'I know. But initially it seemed simpler if she spent her first few years just being with me—and Marina and Soula— as if that was the norm. She doesn't really know how other families function.'

Daggers of pain were zigzagging across her chest. 'She...calls Marina, Mummy?'

He hesitated and she held her breath, aching. 'No,' he said eventually. 'Emma, she's been too young for explanations up to now. I was working up to telling her in due course, but you turned up sooner than I'd imagined. I wasn't expecting you. She's just a baby still, Emma, only just out of nappies. The last thing I want is for her to be disturbed by your arrival. I'm sure you feel that way too and would want to ease your way in gently.'

Her eyes were huge with dismay. This was awful. She'd have a lot of groundwork to do before Lexi felt comfortable with her. It looked as if she'd be staying for some considerable time, because she would not take Lexi back to England until her daughter had grown to love and trust her.

'What are you suggesting?' she asked, searching his face for an answer.

He did seem concerned. His jaw was tight with strain. Perhaps he did care about Lexi. She bit her lip, suddenly on uncertain ground. A false step and her child would be lost to her for ever. She put her fork down with a clatter, misery tugging down the corners of her mouth.

'Emma,' Leon said soothingly. 'I understand how you feel—'

'Do you?' she muttered, flicking up a sullen glance at him.

'I can imagine what it would be like to have a child, who I'd watched over as a baby, asking who I was...'

His voice had cracked. Her quick appraisal told her that his mouth had compressed and that he was valiantly trying to hide a private pain.

Her eyes softened. 'It happened to you, didn't it?' she said gently. 'You were estranged from your own daughter.'

'It...was a different situation.' He growled, apparently more interested in eating.

But Emma could see that swallowing was a problem and she knew herself what that meant. She couldn't eat when emotion had constricted her throat. She felt very tender and protective towards him.

'And how did you resolve it?' she asked softly.

'Who said it was resolved?' The bitterness in his tone was unmistakable. He abandoned his efforts to finish his starter and took a gulp of wine instead. His eyes were raw with anguish. 'I made a mistake, Emma. In my ignorance, I imagined I could walk back into Soula's life and everything would be fine. I couldn't, and it wasn't.' He leaned towards her, his expression fierce. 'I know what happened to that child. So Lexi isn't going to be messed up, not by you or anybody. She's happy and carefree and I will go to hell and back to keep her that way.'

Emma stared in dismay. There were pitfalls in her path that she never knew had existed. 'You know what went wrong with Soula,' she said jerkily. 'So you can make it right, this time.'

'I can.' He removed their plates and carried dishes to the table, waving aside her offer of help. 'This is how we'll do it. I want you to come to the house and be introduced to Lexi as someone her daddy used to know.'

'But...' She stared at him helplessly. He was absorbed in lifting the lid of the casserole dish. An aroma of spices and herbs wafted enticingly in the air but she ignored it. 'You're robbing me of the moment I've dreamed of. She's my *child*—'

'I know.' His hand reached across the table to hers in a consoling gesture but his expression was determined. 'That's why you'll do this.'

'No. I won't—'

'Your needs or hers? You have to choose,' he said fiercely. 'This needs very delicate handling. First you both need to make friends. I don't want you telling her that you are her mother until she's ready.'

He became blurred. She rubbed her eyes till they cleared. 'I don't think I can agree,' she whispered. 'All these years I've waited to hear her call me Mummy.' Her voice shattered.

'I'd look at her with longing and pain,' she said brokenly, 'and everyone would see—'

'I'd be there,' he said quietly. 'No one else.'

'Marina—'

'Is hardly ever around.'

'Soula—'

'Wouldn't notice. She's too concerned with her own problems to be aware of anyone else's.' His hand curled around hers properly, tightly, and she realised how passionately he felt about this. '*Try* it. For Lexi. I'm giving a lot here, Emma. I could fight you over this and force you to apply to the courts and to hell with my reputation. I don't want that. Lexi will be harmed. Come tomorrow. You've waited a long time, I know, to be acknowledged as Lexi's mother. A little while longer won't hurt.'

It would. It would. Her lip trembled. 'Leon, you don't know what you're ask-ask…' Tears backed up in her throat. She looked at him in mute appeal.

His hand slid from hers and stroked the side of her face, stopping her sobs altogether. A rush of longing engulfed her like a tidal wave.

And then they were both staring at his mobile phone, which seemed to be buzzing and jerking around at the far end of the table. Leon said something short and pithy in Greek and stretched out for it.

'*Ne?*' he snapped. His brows zapped together furiously as he listened. 'She's here.' Leon held out the phone. 'Sefton.'

It was a moment before Emma had gathered herself sufficiently to sound vaguely normal. She opted for, 'Hi,' deciding that any more syllables would betray her shakiness.

'I've been going crazy wondering how you are,' complained John petulantly.

'I'm sorry—' she began, immediately contrite.

'Where are you? Do you know what time it is? If you don't get to your digs—'

'I—I've got somewhere to stay,' she mumbled, feeling

horribly guilty. 'John, I totally forgot! I arrived here and fell asleep—'

'Where's here? And what's *he* doing there?'

She could almost hear his lower lip jutting out. 'Leon's let me use a house on his estate,' she explained in a remorseful rush. 'I'm seeing Lexi tomorrow, isn't that wonderful?' She accepted the plate of beef from Leon and nodded her thanks.

'Where? I ought to be there. And where exactly is this house?' John demanded truculently.

'I've no idea. Where are you? Hotel…Zantos.' Hearing Leon's amused snort, she glanced up at him and found herself smiling. 'I'll ring you,' she said drily.

'Let me know when and where to pick you up,' he ordered.

She took a deep breath. 'No, we'll meet later and I'll report on my progress. I'll explain why, when I see you. I have to do this on my own, John. I don't want to rock the boat. Leon's been very accommodating.' Absently she helped herself to rice and vegetables. 'I must go,' she said, cutting across John's protests. 'We're discussing the arrangements. *John*. Listen to me,' she begged. 'Please don't do this to me. It's just that I don't need you for this stage of—'

She blinked and slowly lowered the phone. 'He rang off!' she exclaimed in astonishment.

'He would. Potatoes?' Leon offered politely.

She dug into the crunchy roasted potato slices and added them to her heaped plate. 'I don't understand it,' she said with a frown. 'We've never disagreed before.'

'Maybe,' Leon murmured, sipping his wine reflectively, 'you've always gone along with what he's said. Look, don't worry about it now. We have more pressing things to discuss. Do you accept my suggestion? In the morning, you can walk through the olive grove to my house and we'll have coffee. Lexi will be playing in the garden. Then I'll suggest we go to the beach together. My land runs to the sea and we have a small beach house. It's a very beautiful spot. You'd like to see her swimming, wouldn't you?' he said persuasively.

Unfair, she thought. 'If I say no?'

'Then my gates will be locked to you, and you won't get near her. You will have to take the legal way out. And if you are granted access, I will not make your meetings with Lexi easy.'

It was a grim prospect and the pictures he'd painted were vivid in her head. Watching her daughter playing, seeing her run and laugh...spending the better part of the day with her, larking about in the sea...

She let out a little, quivery breath. His solution couldn't be faulted. And she'd see Lexi in the morning.

'Yes,' she whispered, her face soft with quiet joy. 'I agree.'

The warmth of the food and the wine—had she drunk too much?—was making her feel very mellow and relaxed. Nothing mattered. Only her child.

'Thank you,' he said huskily. 'I knew you'd do what's best for her. To tomorrow.'

'Tomorrow.' she said, her voice low with passion. 'Tomorrow.'

CHAPTER FIVE

HE TOLD her about the island while they ate, his melodious voice and deep love for his homeland slipping effortlessly into her mind, like the heady wine.

'Coffee and brandy outside?' he murmured, when they'd finished the rich, sweet filo pudding. 'Bit of pudding—corner of your mouth,' he added.

Her finger found the sticky blob and her tongue enjoyed the last taste of cinnamon-flavoured honey and walnut.

'Thanks. And outside would be lovely,' she said with a sigh.

Her mind swirled deliciously with magical names: Zeus and Apollo and Aphrodite, Troy, Odysseus and Homer. But it was his own story that had captured her imagination. And she wanted more information about him.

When he opened the door to the garden, the colour of the pool took her breath away for the second time. But now it was lit by underwater lamps and its delicate aquamarine contrasted dramatically with the velvety darkness, which was broken only by the thick scattering of twinkling stars above.

Stepping down to the terrace was like moving into another world. There seemed to be an intense silence over everything, almost weighting the air. And nothing ruffled the extraordinary stillness other than an occasional whirring from a few diffident cicadas or the rustle of a lizard as it moved in the undergrowth.

'It's very peaceful,' she said in a hushed whisper, as they pulled their chairs around to enjoy the view.

'A little different from London,' he replied softly.

Smiling, she sat there, her senses swimming from the incredibly powerful perfume of the roses and thought of ev-

75

erything he'd said, remembering every detail of his impassioned words.

Long ago the Venetians had called Zakynthos the flower of the east, the island of love. In rich and fervent tones Leon had painted pictures for her: the rich greens of the landscape, the olive, pine and cypress trees, the carpets of spring flowers and crystal-clear seas.

He'd spoken of the warm sense of community, the age-old values of courtesy, respect, and hospitality. She could see in her mind's eye the old men sitting over a game of chess in the *kafenion*—the café—and dark-eyed boys herding goats in the mountains. And she looked forward to visiting Zante town and seeing the busy port he'd described with its fishing boats and island ferries chugging back and forth across the sparkling sea.

Even more fascinating, he'd told her how once the beaches in the south had been black with loggerhead turtles, which hauled themselves up to lay over a hundred eggs apiece in the sand, digging shafts with their rear flippers. In answer to her eager questioning, he said that many still came to the beaches where they'd been born and the hatchlings—as small as a child's hand—emerged at night in a helter-skelter dash for the sea. She would like to see that.

Yes. It was different from London. Given time, her soul could recover here, as well as her body, she thought wistfully.

'The tourists who come to this island and this villa will never want to leave,' she mused, feeling envious.

'Then, they will show remarkable good taste,' he said huskily.

Idly she mused that it would be wonderful to live on the island. But that was impossible as far as she was concerned. If she wanted Lexi, she'd have to live in England, out of Leon's clutches.

'You have it all,' she said, lifting her head to inhale the scented breeze.

'No one has it all.'

'John thinks you have,' she said slowly.

Leon grunted. 'He's blind. Beware his advice—'

'You keep denigrating him,' she complained mildly. 'Don't spoil this pleasant evening.' It was more than pleasant, she thought. For the first time in years she felt at ease. And happy. That was because she was close to her goal. 'John's been unbelievably kind to me. I don't know why.'

'Because you're beautiful.'

Astonished, she turned her head to look him full in the face. In the soft lamplight he seemed deadly serious. Her heart bumped unevenly. And she couldn't prevent herself from saying breathlessly, 'Am I?'

'Stunning.'

With an effort he looked elsewhere. He wanted to drink her up: her wide, solemn eyes with their fringe of impossibly long lashes which so often closed in ecstasy; the fine-boned face and its satin skin which he could still feel warm and vibrant beneath his fingers from where he'd dared to touch her earlier; her mass of rich gold hair heaping in scented drifts about her shoulders...

He sucked in a breath. Those silky smooth shoulders! The perfect back, naked to his startled eyes when she'd first turned around. The high mounds of her lush breasts...

There was a tremendous pressure within his chest. She was leaning forwards, her dress falling away from her long, glossy legs. Leon knew he was in trouble when he couldn't locate his brandy glass. Things were happening too rapidly. She was far too sexy and he too hungry.

'Oh, look, Leon,' she whispered furtively, her hand descending on his knee. 'Bats,' she said in breathy excitement.

Bats! Flitting over the pool, dipping like tiny black scimitars to drink... While flames roared inside him, fires consumed him, his head was near to exploding...

And now their gazes had meshed. Electricity shot between them and every muscle and sinew in her body contracted as his did. His arms were around her though how they'd got there he didn't know. Amazingly, her hands were curving around the nape of his neck, drawing him close.

He could manage only the shallowest of breaths, high in his throat. For a second or two they remained frozen in a tense and expectant tableau, postponing the moment their lips met—as surely they would.

But the waiting was delicious, so tormentingly exciting, and he could enjoy the perfection, the fragrance of her skin and hair, the heat of desire leaping from her sultry eyes.

Imperceptibly he inclined his head and her lips parted with a tortured moan. Knowing her as he did, remembering the madness that had descended on them both when they had made love, he closed his eyes briefly and groaned too.

With deceptive gentleness—because his animal instincts were driving him to rip her clothes off and make hot, passionate love to her without pausing for breath—he tipped up her chin.

His finger slipped erotically along the line of her jaw. They looked into one another's eyes and did not speak but their eyes and their bodies spoke for them. Closer and closer his mouth came until it was almost on hers.

Never in the whole of his life had he felt like this. His whole world had become focussed on a woman's lips: lush and full, pouting and trembling, the whiteness of her even teeth startling in the hushed stillness of the night.

A faint touch of her lips. Satin, he thought, and then slowly, thoroughly, he moved his mouth over hers without pressure, reminding himself of its plush curves...

He smiled affectionately. A little stickiness. The tip of his tongue darted out. Honey. He sucked gently at her lower lip, knowing with a growing triumph that she was trembling in his arms as if demons were shaking her.

Up, up to the peaked arch of her upper lip, down and then up again. Sweeping along to tantalise the corner with his tongue. Nothing sweeter.

He rose fluidly and she slithered up his body with him

while his mouth wandered the contours of her slender jaw, his hands cupping her face so that soon his lips could feel the length of that smooth throat where her pulse beat so rapidly.

Still he was gentle, as if hardly daring to unleash his passion. But she was restless and impatient, her hands digging in his hair, tugging his head towards her so that his kisses deepened. She nibbled at his mouth. Began to devour him.

Her body moved lightly against his in a sinuous motion and, as the sleek voluptuousness beneath the thin dress began to make itself known, he found himself close to forgetting everything he'd planned.

She *had* intended seduction, he thought hazily. And then, before he could ask why, his mind fractured as the heat of her loins suddenly flared against the pounding throb of his body.

'Emma,' he breathed helplessly.

'Kiss me. *Hard*,' she moaned.

He cried out in anguish, his voice hoarse and thick, cracking with the choking passion that commanded his senses. With a rough moment, his hand splayed over her tight buttocks and jerked her into him while his mouth descended on hers in a ruthlessly driving kiss that obliterated everything from his mind but their two bodies and the explosive longing which would not be denied.

Yes, this was how it used to be. Her sighs, her eagerness, the drowsy flutter of her curling lashes, the instinctive lure of her wickedly enticing mouth. The feel of her hands on his chest and shoulders as if they were loving the shape of him, and which made him feel a giant among men. The rising tension between them, driven by demanding hands and lips, the desperation, oh, the sweet desperation to taste and touch and know every inch of one another's bodies...

Her fingers tugged at his shirt buttons, then his impatient, impulsive and passionate Emma, her face beautiful in its frustrated anger, gripped both edges and ripped the shirt open to her avid greed.

He felt her soft cheek rest on his chest, looked down with dazed eyes, saw the gentle curve of her face against his bronzed skin and then watched with mounting, sweet agony as her mouth began to explore.

Shaking, he reached around to her back, letting memories return. Vaguely he registered that the strong rope of muscles on either side of her spine was less pronounced now but her skin was still flawless to his trailing caress.

The tie at her waist came undone easily. Just up to her nape now and when that bow was undone he'd have her breasts in his trembling hands.

'No!'

Emma wriggled in his grasp, cold reality suddenly descending. She couldn't. Wanted to, yes. *Yes!* But...

'No, Leon,' she rasped, when he continued to tussle with the tie at her neck.

She put her hands up. Peeled off a surprised finger or two. Met his bewildered, hazy eyes and wanted to weep. Her body screamed at her, wanting, starving for his magic touch.

It had been so good, she mourned. No...more than that, it had seemed as if her heart was being healed.

'No,' she moaned.

His hands fell away. He stood there thrusting shaking fingers through his tousled hair, the dark curls dancing angrily on his frowning forehead. She took a step back and then another, her eyes averted from that smooth and golden torso which her hands had caressed only a few wonderful moments ago.

'Why?' he said gratingly.

She bit her lip and found it was trembling. Because there was an ugly dent in her breast, a savage scar. She feared his disgust and that was something she wasn't strong enough to bear yet.

Suddenly he was walking away, back up the steps to the

villa, each stride thundering his anger. You don't do this to men, she thought miserably. They never forgive you.

'Leon, please...'

He paused, waiting for her explanation, his body language explicit in its tense fury. Then, when she struggled for an excuse, he whirled, his eyes slashing like swords in the darkness of his face.

'A game, was it?' he rasped. 'Get me excited, lure me on, push me away, get me in your power... Oh, come on, Emma,' he yelled, beyond anger, almost out of control, 'I'm not a kid you can play around with. This isn't Taki, or Sefton, hanging on your every word, turning somersaults to please you—'

'I—I'm sorry, I didn't mean... It got out of...hand—' She choked.

He erupted, cursed in Greek, the words hurtling through his teeth. And then he smashed his fist into the palm of his hand as if furious with himself. She could see the effort it was costing him to rein in his temper. The line of his mouth was hard and vicious, his jaw rock-solid.

With scant regard for his shirt, he almost punched it back into place. She saw the absence of buttons and dropped her eyes guiltily, horrified by the violence of her passion.

'I don't like being teased,' he growled dangerously.

She gulped. 'It wasn't like that.'

'How was it then?' He shot the words vehemently.

For the life of her, she didn't know. Other than frightening in its intensity, the terrible loss of conscious thought, the way she'd lurched headlong into a seething cauldron of lust and sensation.

'I've no idea,' she croaked, her eyes glistening.

For long, painful seconds, which ticked by in an agony of suspense, he glowered at her as if promising a murderous revenge. And then he turned on his heel again and ran up the steps.

He couldn't comprehend what had happened, only that he

had to get away before he said any more. She'd been close to surrender, his goal almost within his grasp, and then...

Heaven help him. He paused, standing stock still in appalled silence. He'd forgotten why he'd broken his self-imposed celibacy. And if Emma wasn't intending to succumb and prove herself to be unsuitably loose, then he had to come up with some other way of protecting Lexi.

His brain wouldn't function. All he could think of was the devastating sense of loss when she'd drawn back and refused him. He stared bleakly at the door, paralysed as he relived her erotic caresses, feeling the tautness in his body as every nerve sprang to life again and tortured him with what might have been.

He hated her. He hated himself.

For several seconds, Emma remained in stunned silence, horrified by the destruction she'd caused by letting go of her inhibitions. Her brain only jerked into operation again when the back door slammed in the breeze behind her.

In panic, she raced after Leon, skidding across the marble floor in her desperation to head him off before he stormed out.

'Leon!' Gasping for breath, she flung herself bruisingly against the front door, her arms outstretched to bar his way. '*What about Lexi?*' she wailed wretchedly.

'Oh, now you think of her, do you? Yourself first, her somewhere far down your order of priorities... My God, Emma,' he said exploding, 'you really are selfish, aren't you? All you think about are your own needs, your own games of power play. It didn't occur to your scheming little mind that I might take offence at being dangled on the end of a line, and refuse to let you see her.'

'No,' she moaned, limp with despair. Her tormented eyes begged. She caught his arm but he flung her hand off as if it had scalded him. 'Don't do this to me—'

'There are several things I'd like to do to you,' he said icily, 'all of them unspeakable.'

He reached out, his expression menacing, and pulled her to his body, crushing her against him so firmly that she could feel his hard, taut muscles and the pulse of his arousal against her pelvis. She dragged in a strangled breath and he gave a mocking smile then lowered his mouth to take hers in a punishing display of contempt.

Then he let her go. And, insultingly, wiped the back of his hand across his mouth.

They were panting hard and fast, shocked by where their passions had taken them, hating, wanting, prevented from fully releasing the dangerous emotions that had been ignited.

She knew that. He knew that. It scared them both, this uncontrollable hunger that took no account of its consequences.

She could hardly stand. Her fist was at her stinging mouth, holding back the screech within her.

'Move aside,' he hissed, dark and feral and more menacing than anyone or anything she'd ever known.

'But...Lexi,' she whispered brokenly. It stuck in her throat to beg. But beg she must. 'Tell me I can still...' She cringed. His eyes had blazed with fury. 'Let me see her,' she whimpered in a small, tinny voice.

He seemed to be thinking rapidly but it was several nerve-racking seconds before he came to some conclusion and by then her mind was in shreds.

'Why not?' He bit out the words, to her utter surprise. He took a stride forward and had caught her jaw in one hand before she could blink. 'But the situation is different now,' he said, growling softly, his breath hot and harsh on her face.

And she flinched as if it scalded her. 'D-d-different?' she stammered.

'You will see her. You will see more than you would wish. You will learn how happy she is, how this island is her home and that she would die of misery anywhere else. You will see how much she loves me and you will suffer, Emma. You will suffer because you will realise that she doesn't need you and doesn't want you and that her life will be all the better if you never tell her who you are, if she never knows for the rest of her life that she is your daughter!'

Released, she crumpled to the floor, all the bones in her body useless. The door closed very quietly behind Leon and as she lay curled in a despairing heap, she heard his car driving away.

The pain made her double up. Holding her lurching stomach, she tried to find the strength to stand but could only manage to crawl towards the nearest chair.

Sobs racked her body. She had made a terrible mistake and her longed-for meeting with Lexi had been ruined, perhaps with fatal results.

Her mouth tightened. OK. She'd tell him why she'd refused him. Let him pick the bones out of that. Hauling herself into the carved seat, she reflected gloomily that he'd probably think she was angling for the sympathy vote. And it wouldn't make any difference. His pride had been dented and he was raring for a fight, looking for a chance to lash out at her in revenge.

No. Wild horses wouldn't drag it out of her that she'd been self-conscious about her damaged breast. Let him think what he liked. She wasn't going to discuss something so personal and life-shattering with anyone, let alone Leon.

But he'd scared her with what he'd said. If Lexi was happy, if... Oh, yes, she thought in dismay, she could see that any child would prefer to live here and not London...

Hot, stinging tears burned like scalding water in her eyes and ran down her cheeks unchecked. Miserably she sopped them up with her tongue, little sobs breaking through her parted lips.

She was horribly afraid that what she had to offer Lexi was not enough. And yet John had been so sure that Leon resented looking after Lexi.

In a gesture of despair, her arms flopped over the arms of

the chair and her left hand hit something hard. She blinked. A telephone.

Perhaps if she could talk this over with someone—a second opinion... She sat up, struggling to compose herself. And after a while she picked up the receiver and dialled with shaky fingers.

'John! It's me, Emma,' she mumbled when a curt voice answered. 'I—I'd like to talk to you... I was wondering...could you come round? *Please?*'

Leon sat on the gnarled and twisted bole of an olive tree which had been the felled victim of an ancient storm, its branches still miraculously thick with leaf and flower. Olives were tough. They took everything the climate could throw at them and still bore fruit. He wished he could be so certain of his own strength.

He didn't dare get in the car again. For the first hundred yards he'd driven on adrenaline and then had realised he'd swerved off the road twice, his tyres biting into the irrigated soil which had played merry hell with the gleaming bodywork.

He'd kill himself if he drove home. And she wasn't worth that...whatever her delights, and they were many.

So he'd abandoned the car and had set about calming himself down, refusing to think about the passion that had swallowed him whole and had turned the tables so disastrously on him.

It had never been his intention to let Emma see Lexi if he could possibly avoid it. He had meant to be seduced. To declare then to the courts that this woman had not only committed fraud but that she'd slept with her brother-in-law the first night she'd arrived on the island. And he would have asked for an injunction to stop her seeing Lexi.

It had been a brutal and morally suspect ploy on his part perhaps, but it would have given Lexi the ultimate protection. And it had rebounded on him—big-time.

He ground his teeth together. Because he'd lost his head, he would now have to spend hours in Emma's company and watch her yearning to hold her daughter. Far from giving him a malicious pleasure, the prospect filled him with dread.

He took a deep breath and his nostrils were immediately assailed by wild honeysuckle and orange blossom. When his foot stirred the rich, red earth he felt suddenly overwhelmed by the love of his land and it swelled to fill his aching heart.

This had been Kyriakis land for generations. And, after him, it would belong to Lexi. He stilled. Sefton had let slip that Emma was determined to take Lexi back to England one way or another. Leon's jaw tightened. That was his worst fear. But his Lexi had her roots here and she must never live anywhere else.

Emma must be persuaded to go home. There was no other way. The ends would justify the means.

Determined on his course, he set off on foot for home. It was then that he heard a car coming up the lane to the villa. Suspecting who it might be, he hurried grimly through the trees and watched with growing anger as the car came to a jerking halt.

Emma emerged from the villa, her face white in the glare of the porch light. She spoke to John Sefton in a low voice and he replied.

Leon heard her utter a low cry. And then Sefton pulled her boldly into his arms.

CHAPTER SIX

IF SHE'D been in a different mood, she would have loved the walk to the house through the olive grove the next morning. John had been wonderful, comforting her into the small hours of the morning and advising her to persevere. His confidence had given her strength and after sleeping late she felt more optimistic and better able to cope.

But she was unbelievably nervous. In a sleeveless blue top and white shorts, with a cheerful pink rucksack on her back, she set off along the path to find Leon's house. She felt as if she were about to take an exam, her stomach churning uncomfortably. And when her footfalls stirred up the scent of mint and basil she gave only a passing thought to them instead of revelling in their combining scents.

Lexi was uppermost in her mind. It terrified her that her daughter wouldn't like her, or would pick up Leon's hatred and be suspicious—perhaps scared.

She'd spent long hours in prison learning Greek but repeating phrases to a tape recorder was a lot different to interpreting a child's chatter, especially with Leon possibly muttering vile things about her under his breath.

She winced. He wanted to make her suffer. All because his sexual pride had been wounded. Men! she thought darkly.

'I will get the better of him,' she muttered, scowling at the herby path.

But the way ahead had changed. The path had widened. She looked up and saw the ground rising gradually. And on a hill, perhaps half a mile away, sat a beautiful, old stone mansion, perfectly proportioned and graceful.

She stared at it wide-eyed. Doubts chased through her

87

mind. To live here, in this paradise, in a beautiful period house, would be any child's dream.

She frowned, thinking positively. If that child wasn't loved, then a cosy cottage somewhere in England and an adoring mother would be better. She'd buy a little house with the remainder of her stash of money. In the country. With chickens.

With that decided, she walked towards the house. Close to, it was very impressive, with Grecian pediments and huge shutters flanking the tall windows. And on the ground floor, French doors lay open to the cooling breeze.

Sick with nerves, she rang the bell and was admitted by a long-legged beauty in jeans and T-shirt. Emma gaped. This wasn't Marina! Some other female, a temporary 'auntie' for her child? she thought, choking with fury.

'Hello. Are you Emma?' asked Long Legs solemnly in an enchanting accent.

'I am,' Emma replied grumpily, sounding anything but enchanting.

'Come.'

The tall, willowy young woman swayed across a high and airy marbled hall, her easy manner in the expensive surroundings crushing Emma's self-confidence still further. It was a long walk. Eventually they reached the back of the house where Long Legs pointed through the open double doors.

'He's in the garden,' she said succinctly to Emma. And swept off, every step disapproving.

Emma's heart sank as she stepped onto the terrace. If everyone around Leon behaved like that towards her, then it would be impossible to convince Lexi that she was harmless.

Pale and trembling, she scanned the fabulous garden and quickly identified Leon, sitting beneath the shade of a rubber tree.

Her hand flew to her mouth to stifle her sharp intake of breath. *There was Lexi.*

A rush of tears clouded her view and she brushed them

away impatiently. 'Oh, sweetheart,' she whispered softly, a catch in her anguished voice. 'Oh, my darling, darling baby.'

With hunger in her heart she watched the sturdy little figure, dressed in a sweet little flowery top and matching shorts which came down to her dimpled knees. Love spilled from Emma's entire being. Someone had put Lexi's hair up in a pony-tail and had fastened it with a bright pink scrunchie but rebellious curls danced all around Lexi's small face.

Emma's heart melted. Her daughter was quite exceptionally beautiful. She let out a soft breath and felt a little better about the meeting. Love would bind them and break down all barriers.

With glazed eyes she watched her daughter happily arranging rose petals in a wooden truck: small piles of pink, white, red, and yellow. Emma felt a pang of pride that little Lexi should be so deeply absorbed in her sorting game, playing with an admirable concentration.

The need to run forwards and crush her sweet baby in her arms was unbearable. So she pressed her lips together and stayed silent behind a column, giving herself a chance to watch unobserved and to yearn openly for her child. Because soon she'd have to appear friendly but detached. Towards her own daughter! Emma's lip trembled at the injustice of that.

Her loving gaze saw the breeze ruffle the rose petals and ruin the neat piles and she smiled in motherly sympathy at Lexi's look of dismay.

'Daddeee!' Lexi wailed in English.

She gasped in horror, ice freezing her spine. Both Leon and Lexi whirled around and Emma hastily hid her face, gripping the pillar with rigid fingers, her head pressed hard against the cold unmoving stone.

'Oh, God!' she moaned, when she heard Leon's quick stride coming up the steps towards her.

'How long have you been there?' he growled, keeping his voice low so it didn't carry to Lexi's ears.

She flung him a furious glance. 'Long enough. She...she calls you *Daddy*! How dare you? In how many ways do you want to take my child from me?' she hurled back in a barely controlled undertone.

'I correct her,' he said quietly, his eyes cold and distant. 'But she persists. She has a mind of her own—as you'll find out.'

'What do you mean? Have you said something detrimental about me?' she demanded, her face hot with anger.

'I've said nothing. I wouldn't waste my breath talking about you. Well, are you ready? I suggest you find a more charming expression.'

With an effort she checked her temper. This was it. The moment she'd been waiting for. Her heartbeat thundered in her ears and the sick sensation coiled hotly in her stomach.

'I—I'm ready. Just one thing, Leon,' she said, her blue eyes wide with apprehension. She moistened her parched lips. 'You must give me a fair crack of the whip. If I suspect even for a moment that you're trying to influence Lexi's opinion of me, then I'm off to see John. I'll get the lawyers involved. Lexi must be given the opportunity to know and love her own mother. Do I make myself clear?'

'Crystal.' His eyes glittered. 'I imagine this is what you and Sefton talked about last night?'

She was taken aback. 'Umm...yes.'

'And this morning?' he enquired sarcastically. 'Or was he helping you with some other, more personal, service?'

She flushed, well aware of what he was implying. 'Do you do your own snooping, or do you get minions to do it for you?' she asked scathingly.

He smiled but it wasn't anywhere near humorous. 'Your evasion has answered my question. Just consider this, Emma. It's a mistake for a woman in your position to put herself about. Me, Sefton, who next, I wonder? Your life needs to be close to sainthood. Anything less and the odds shorten against you.'

Emma met his glittering eyes coolly even though she was registering the truth of what he was saying. She would have to be very careful. John had insisted on staying till she fell asleep. It had been a wonderful gesture but he knew she was under surveillance and he should have realised that Leon would misinterpret the situation.

'I have nothing on my conscience,' she said, her chin high. 'And now I want to meet my daughter.'

He frowned. 'You remember what we agreed?'

He was barring her way. He'd turn her away if necessary, even now. 'Yes, yes, I'm to say I knew her daddy,' she said in a choking voice. 'I'll keep to my side of the bargain—but no tricks on your part,' she warned.

He smiled again, his eyes bright and hard. 'I won't need any.'

Emma shivered. He seemed so confident. He raised his hand to attract someone's attention in the house and Long Legs glided silently to his side.

'Would you bring some coffee, Natasa?' he asked pleasantly.

Natasa dimpled. 'Of course. And freshly squeezed orange for Lexi? I have some biscuits I made this morning if you're interested...' She paused and raised a shapely eyebrow in query, sharing some private joke with Leon.

His eyes crinkled with laughter as he ruefully patted his flat stomach and Emma found herself gritting her teeth, uncharitably wishing that Natasa would vanish off the face of the earth. Emma couldn't translate his reply and that infuriated her even further, but it was evidently funny because they both fell into fits of giggles.

'Obliging girl,' Emma found herself saying sarcastically, like some jealous wife. She went pink with fury at herself. What did she care *how* obliging Natasa was?

'She's hell-bent on single-handedly altering my waistline by cooking like an angel.' Leon's face sobered as he gazed after the pendulum swing of Natasa's rear. Emma clenched her fists hard. 'She is a gem. A diamond among women.'

'Pearl,' she corrected shortly. 'It's pearl.'

'Not in this case. Diamonds are for ever.'

She felt her heart bump unevenly. 'Are you trying to tell me something?' she asked as coolly as humanly possible. 'Is Natasa likely to be a permanent fixture in my daughter's life?'

'Anastasia—Natasa—is welcome to stay here as long as she wishes,' Leon answered quietly.

What was he doing, she wondered in amazement, operating a harem? Against her better wishes, she imagined him coming home last night, angry and sexually frustrated—and hated to think of what might have happened next between him and the nubile Natasa.

'I hope she's nice to Lexi,' she muttered.

'Brilliant. Come and discover how happy your daughter is,' he goaded. She hurled a glare at him as they walked down the steps into the landscaped garden. 'Lexi,' he called gently. She looked up, glanced at Emma and continued to rearrange the rose petals with a frown of concentration on her small forehead. 'This is someone your real daddy knew in England.'

Emma held her breath, a smile frozen on her nervous face. 'Hello,' she said, speaking in Greek like Leon. She was pleased at his look of surprise.

Lexi gave her an old-fashioned stare and returned to her game. Emma gulped in disappointment. But what had she expected? Some kind of psychic recognition, and her daughter beaming at her in joy and running up for a hug? She sucked in a shaky breath. The answer, stupidly, was yes.

Leon was smiling smugly and easing himself into the comfortable cane chair. Emma marshalled her wits and went to kneel on the lawn beside Lexi, her hands gripped tightly together so she wouldn't do anything silly like grab hold of her daughter and frighten her witless by clutching her to her heart.

'I have a present for you,' she said lovingly in her carefully rehearsed Greek.

Lexi looked up from beneath dark Kyriakis lashes. And went back to sorting the petals. Emma's heart beat hard but she bided her time. This was a child not to be bought. It didn't matter—on the contrary, it showed great strength of character, she rationalised.

Patiently Emma waited and watched. She noted that Lexi's fingers were surprisingly dextrous. She didn't get that from Taki. He'd been clumsy. Her eyes shifted to Leon's hands which were long and slender and capable of great delicacy of touch and she was glad that her daughter had inherited that particular Kyriakis trait.

Emma ached with longing and it was taking all her bitterly learnt self-control to remain physically neutral. Lexi was so deeply engrossed, so utterly sweet. Any mother would have caught her up and hugged her breathless by now—but she wasn't any mother. She was on trial and this trial would have far-reaching consequences.

Casually she slid off her rucksack and began to undo the clasps, knowing Lexi was watching surreptitiously. Emma's fingers fumbled because they were shaking so much and she gave Leon an imploring look.

'You're on your own,' he drawled.

Then she felt a small, soft hand on hers and froze. Lexi was helping! Emma felt a huge rush of emotion to be so close to her child, to see the fair hairs gleaming on the smooth brow, the stubby little nose wrinkled in concentration... She couldn't *bear* it, she thought with an inner groan. This was torture...

Lexi moved back, the clasps undone and Emma frantically eased her tense muscles and gave her daughter a radiant smile.

'Thank you,' she said warmly, and searched her limited

vocabulary. 'You are clever!' she exclaimed. 'Look, this is what I have for you.'

She drew out the smaller pink rucksack and placed it in front of Lexi who looked at it uncertainly then checked with Leon—but his attention was fixed on something he'd seen to his right.

'Thank you very much,' Lexi said politely.

But Emma could see she was pleased. Already the contents were being investigated. Lexi lifted out the soft fabric doll and immediately took off the sun hat and peeled off the Velcro that held the dress fast. Underneath was a shocking pink bikini. Lexi beamed in pleasure.

Emma leaned forwards, hardly daring to breathe, and pointed out that the rucksack on the doll's back contained toy sun cream, a hairbrush, towel, sunglasses and flowery mules for the doll.

'Oh!' Lexi squealed excitedly and it was as if Emma had won a million pounds.

But then Lexi ran to Leon to show him and Emma bit her lip, forcing herself to remember that she was a stranger and a hug would have been most unlikely.

The doll was being investigated and the bikini was already half-off. Leon solemnly received the hairbrush and followed orders to tidy the yellow wool plaits, while Lexi persevered with the difficult task of fixing the sunglasses securely.

'You like it?' Emma ventured brightly.

But Lexi didn't look at her, she was too taken up with dabbing the sun cream bottle all over the doll's body.

Leon met Emma's tormented eyes. 'Go and say thank you nicely,' he prompted Lexi in a growly voice.

Her daughter put her arms around Leon's neck and cuddled him. That hurt Emma more than she could have believed possible. Her daughter loved someone else more than she loved *her*.

'Go on,' he urged.

'Thank you,' Lexi said solemnly to Emma, having scrambled down from Leon's lap.

'You're welcome,' she replied jerkily.

'Emma, come and have coffee.' Leon's dark eyes were upon her, their expression unreadable when she was expecting mocking triumph.

Feeling dispirited, she jumped up and sat in the chair he'd indicated as Natasa brought a tray to them.

'Thanks, 'Tasa. Aren't you stopping with us?' he asked in surprise, seeing that she'd laid the tray for just two people.

Natasa smiled fondly. 'Not today, Leon. I am making *tiropitta*.'

Amiably she stroked Lexi's bent head and the little girl looked up with a beaming smile that made Emma wince. There was another exchange between Natasa and Leon that was teasing and familiar, which ended with Natasa pretending to threaten Leon with the coffee pot.

Emma watched, isolated by their friendship, bewildered that she should be upset when Leon sat back and gazed after Natasa with a tiger-got-the-cream smile on his face.

'Right,' he said, grabbing the coffee pot. 'Lexi, up to the table, please.'

'Can't she stay there, playing?' Emma asked, seeing her daughter's reluctance.

'No,' he replied firmly. 'She must sit at a table if she wants to eat.'

'But—'

'There are no buts,' he said. 'That is the rule in this house.'

And to her surprise, Lexi meekly gave the doll a kiss, laid it down and clambered up to the chair that Leon was holding out for her.

'Good girl,' Leon said approvingly and was rewarded with a seraphic smile.

'Please-may-I-have-a-biscuit?' Lexi asked all in one breath.

'Certainly—uh...*one*!' he instructed in a shocked tone.

Lexi's hand hovered and Emma hid a smile as her daughter locked frowning stares with Leon, searching for any sign of weakness. He didn't waver. Unfazed, the little girl placed the one biscuit on her plate and broke it in half.

'Two,' she said perkily.

Leon pressed his lips together to stop himself laughing. 'I never really win,' he muttered to himself.

'I'm so glad,' Emma said drily. 'Lexi,' she went on with a fond smile, 'what will you call your dolly?'

The startling blue eyes regarded her steadily. 'Mama,' she said.

Emma choked on her biscuit. Leon slapped her on the back and put a glass of iced water in her hand.

'It's a temporary obsession,' he explained curtly in English. 'She wants to be like Soula.'

Lexi began to chat to Leon. Her conversation was so quick and occasionally garbled that Emma couldn't understand what she was saying. But her daughter was laughing and she could tell that the two of them were fond of one another and were at ease in each other's company.

Leon was ever watchful, she noticed, seeing problems before they arose. Without making a song and a dance about it, he moved Lexi's colourful plastic cup away from her exuberantly gesturing hands. Her daughter was impetuous and enthusiastic, she mused. Just like her.

And a moment later he heaved his wriggling niece back to the centre of her chair when it seemed she might fall off in her excitement.

He also gently asked her to slow down her frantic gobbling of her biscuit. Just like her, Emma thought again—she always ate fast. Her father had said she seemed eager to grab life by the throat—or teeth—and never did anything slowly.

'Did you like your biscuit?' Leon enquired of Lexi.

'Mmm-*mmm*!' she said. 'Did you?'

He grinned. 'I think we'd all like another one. Yes?'

Lexi clapped her hands. 'Yes, please!'

Emma was interested to see that he was a stickler for good manners, making sure that Lexi never spoke with her mouth full nor interrupted a conversation. She wasn't sure she would have been so strict with such a young child but her daughter seemed to be coping very well with the rules.

Perhaps, Emma thought gloomily, that was because he doted on Lexi and she on him. His body language told her that. And the expression on his face when he looked at the little girl was tenderness itself.

Emma felt utterly excluded by their mutual affection. This was no act for her benefit, nor to punish her. It was obvious that he had become both father and mother to her daughter. Hence his opposition to anyone who might take one of those roles away from him.

John had made a terrible mistake. She shrank into her seat, hardly noticing that the coffee was almost scalding her mouth. Leon adored her child. And that was why he'd felt confident in inviting her here.

She couldn't have spoken if she'd wanted to. She knew she'd gone pale, that tremors were capturing her body and draining it of strength. Her lips seemed glued together; dry and bloodless, arcing down in misery.

Lexi's sturdy little legs were swinging beneath the table. Leon caught one in his hand while he replied to something she'd said and his hand affectionately stroked the soft, baby skin.

Emma closed her eyes at witnessing such casual intimacy, the kind usually shown only between fond parent and daughter. He has claimed her for his own, she thought miserably, her heart bumping hard in her chest. *My child!*

'Emma. Are you all right?' Leon asked quietly in English.

'No,' she whispered.

'Do you want to go back to the villa, or do you want to come to the beach with us?' he asked gruffly.

'I—I'll come to the beach,' she mumbled.

'Sure? Haven't you had enough?' Leon queried. 'I think

I'd better rescue that.' He took the coffee cup from her shaking hands and she stared at it with blank eyes. 'Emma, this won't get any easier for you... Lex, if you've finished,' he said, breaking off, 'you can go and play. Let me wipe your mouth.'

Emma's heart lurched as he took out a handkerchief and delicately wiped the little mouth which had been pursed up in preparation for the ritual.

'Kiss!' Lexi demanded merrily.

'Sweetheart,' he murmured, gently kissing each rosy cheek.

Emma writhed and caught a fragment of something that Lexi was saying about love.

'Yes,' Leon answered huskily, his forefinger tucking a golden curl behind Lexi's small ear. 'I love you, poppet.'

Emma looked away, unable to bear any more.

'Listen to me,' Leon said softly in her ear. His low tone made her skin tingle. 'Don't do this to yourself. You've had long enough to see that your daughter is fit and well and very happy—'

'And she is loved,' Emma whispered miserably.

'Very much.' He sounded very gentle, almost as if he knew how badly she was hurting. But that couldn't be so. His only concern was for Lexi. 'Why did you put yourself through this?' he asked. 'You must have known that after two years with me her life would be established. I am her legal guardian. I have pledged to devote myself to her.'

She turned glistening eyes to him. 'I didn't think it would be like this. You—you gave John the impression that she was a nuisance,' she mumbled, choking over the words.

'That's not true.' He hesitated, glanced down at Lexi who was politely tapping his knee for attention, and he tied the ribbon which had come unknotted around the doll's improbably yellow hair. 'Either he's a terrible judge of character, or he was determined to think ill of me, or...or he wanted you to come here and be disappointed.'

'Why would he do that?' she said indignantly.

Leon shrugged. 'Perhaps,' he said, his eyes dark and watchful, 'he likes to be needed and he hoped you'd run to him for comfort.'

'I wouldn't...' Her voice tailed away. She had done just that. And John had seemed delighted, smiling as he'd soothed her, had stroked her back, and had held her tightly... She bit her lip, determined not to be thrown off course. 'Lexi must get to know me,' she said obstinately.

'Why? Don't you think she can live happily without you?'

Emma glared. 'Maybe now she can, but soon she'll want to know who her mother is,' she declared. 'She's already muddled, calling you daddy and naming her doll "Mama". That's not normal, Leon. She wants to be like Soula, who knows very well who she is and who her parents are.'

Leon winced. Soula was also muddled—Marina had seen to that. But Emma had a point. Lexi's searching for a parent was beginning to present a problem. The last thing he wanted was for her to end up an emotional mess like Soula. And keeping Emma out of the equation was surely the best solution. He could then deal with the problem quietly and lovingly, without Emma's emotional input.

He shuddered. He certainly didn't want anyone else having hysterics in the house. He'd had enough to last a lifetime.

'I understand what you're saying,' he said, 'but this is clearly painful for you—'

'I've been through pain before. And fear, and humiliation,' she cried passionately.

Her words reached deep inside him, wounding him as though she'd wielded a knife. Looking deeply into her eyes, he could see the scars of her life there, raw and naked and slashing across the clear blueness like a laser. Her lashes had become spiked with tears and her mouth had parted softly, the swelling curve of her lips trembling gently with misery.

Reluctant to let her into their lives, he suppressed his overwhelming sense of compassion and raked in a strangled breath.

'Then, why suffer any more?' he argued. 'Be glad she's safe. And go home.'

Emma moaned. It was tempting. To shut him out, this house, Lexi's happy face... To start her life again... There would be certain torment if she stayed. And her planned abduction was looking less and less likely with every second that passed.

But the moment she considered the idea of leaving, she knew she couldn't do it. There would be something unfinished about her life. At least if she tried to befriend Lexi and failed, she would know where she was, once and for all.

'I can't go without being acknowledged as Lexi's mother,' she said croakily. 'I know it'll be hard for me. But it's her right to know me. It's not much to ask, Leon, access to my own daughter.'

His eyes narrowed. 'But is that *all* you want?'

Caught off guard, her eyes flashed to his and revealed the truth. His sympathetic expression vanished. 'I—I'd expect to have her for holidays when she's old enough—' she began honestly, hoping to cover up her secret intentions.

'While she is still under age, she will never leave Zakynthos without me,' Leon said meaningfully.

'Then, I will claim my rights in court,' she said defiantly.

He looked over at Lexi, who was happily stuffing rose petals into the doll's rucksack. 'You'll be wasting your money—and Sefton ought to know that. Go to an independent lawyer here and learn the truth,' he said in a hard tone. 'The situation is this, Emma. She is under my care. You will be able to visit a couple of times a year—'

'I want more than that!' she cried.

'Then, you will have to live on this island. That was the ruling in the case of a friend of mine who was having similar problems with his German ex-wife. She had to give up her home and her job in Germany and come to live on Zakynthos. Or never see her children again.'

CHAPTER SEVEN

EMMA sat quietly, watching Leon reading a bed-time story to Lexi, her mind in turmoil. It could have been an idyllic day if the shadow of her daughter's future hadn't hung over everything they did.

They had taken a picnic to the beach below the house, walking through the glorious gardens which were alive with birdsong and thick with the scent of plant oils vaporising in the heat.

Dancing ahead of them, her daughter had looked the picture of happiness. Occasionally Leon had called out and the little girl had come running eagerly, to be shown delights: a gecko with its padded feet, tadpoles in a meandering stream, a snake's skull, and—most exciting—a huge eel lurking in a pond beneath a huge eucalyptus.

Each time Emma had bitten back her urge to be the one who expanded Lexi's knowledge of the world around her. But Leon had been able to explain in fluent Greek, of course, and she'd had to ask him to translate nearly everything he'd said.

Language had proved to be just one more barrier. Until Lexi unexpectedly had spoken in English.

'Marina was born and brought up in England,' Leon had said a little uncomfortably. 'She and Soula speak mainly English. Lexi will probably grow up bilingual—she has as many English words as Greek.'

It had been easier after that. She'd said nothing but had given Leon a hard, angry glare and had spent the rest of the afternoon concentrating solely on Lexi, building sandcastles, digging a pit for the sea to fill, and running squealing in and

101

out of the waves with her. Their shared laughter had been worth a thousand tears.

And once, she'd even lifted her daughter in her arms when a huge wave from the wash of a boat had rolled towards them. For a brief, glorious moment she had held the firm little body close, Lexi's excited giggle tickling her ear.

Then had come the demand to be put down and she'd had to comply, her arms suddenly horribly empty of her wriggling, much wanted burden.

As Leon finished the story and kissed Lexi's sleepy face, hot tears prickled in Emma's eyes, but she refused to cry again. The day had been full of bitter-sweetness and yet the joy had exceeded the sadness.

And now it was late, very late. Lexi had been determined to keep going till she was ready to drop and, because Emma was there, Leon had let her. However, she knew this was part of his plan for her to be convinced of Lexi's happiness.

Her daughter had certainly co-operated in that plan. That afternoon Lexi had refused to take a nap on the beach, but had consented to curl up on Leon's naked chest for a few minutes.

Sighing with envy, Emma had stared at them both: her daughter's small body squirreled into a ball, Leon's tanned and muscular length stretched out on a lounger beneath a huge sunshade.

Emma's throat had gone dry. It had been the most tender and heart-wrenching picture and she had found herself wishing fruitlessly that he was Lexi's father, not Taki.

Because his eyes had been closed, she had been free to feast her gaze on his tousled dark hair, which was breaking the line of his broad forehead. She had admired the beautiful jut of his strong nose, the carved arch of his mouth, and the power of his perfectly toned body.

And then Lexi: sweet-faced, pouting-lipped and infinitely adorable, lying so trustingly in Leon's adoring embrace. Her daughter would be safe with him. He would bring her up well.

Emma had turned away, fighting the sharp pain which had knifed through her chest. *She* adored Lexi. *She* would bring her up safe and well! And Lexi was flesh of her flesh, blood of her blood.

A grunt had interrupted her thoughts. Lexi had scrambled up and was bouncing on Leon's hard stomach till he'd lifted her off. Emma and Leon had exchanged amused glances at Lexi's desire not to miss a second of the day.

Emma sighed. She remembered the catch in her throat at the sight of her daughter at the water's edge, as she'd picked up handfuls of sand and had happily thrown them into the glittering waves. Funny little mite! she'd thought affectionately.

'Night, Lex,' Leon murmured, bringing Emma back to the present.

The little hand opened and closed in a heart-wrenchingly sweet attempt at a wave. 'Night.'

'Say goodnight to Emma,' he prompted.

'Goodnight to Emma,' Lexi obediently, wickedly, replied and they all chuckled.

'Goodnight, Lexi,' Emma said huskily, her voice shaking with emotion as her daughter pushed the new doll under the bedclothes. And she turned to leave.

'Night Mama.'

Emma froze, every nerve in her body electrified. Leon too, was visibly shaken. Slowly she swivelled back again, a smile lighting her face, her heart soaring with delight. It had happened!

And then, through her glistening tears of happiness, she saw that Lexi was hugging and kissing the doll. *Mama*.

Leon couldn't move for shock. Seeing Emma's joy and disappointment had shaken him more than he could have believed possible. And now, with a cold certainty, he realised that Lexi was showing the first outward signs of deprivation.

Appalled, he registered Emma's white face, heard her broken sob and felt his body turn to ice when she ran from the room as if the hounds of hell were after her.

He passed a hand over his forehead, rooted to the spot. Lexi's need for her own mother and father had only become apparent in the last ten days. But for a child of that age, ten days was a long time. He muttered a low curse. Events had escalated faster than he'd dreamed. He needed to take action—fast.

Emma ran out of steam halfway down the stairs. Incapable of continuing, she slumped in a miserable heap on one of the wide steps. Leon came to sit beside her. His whole body was tense for some reason and she gritted her teeth, so exhausted—both emotionally and physically—that she couldn't bear to do battle with him.

All she wanted was to be spirited back to the villa by some magic hand, to be presented with a cup of tea and then carried to bed. She felt she could sleep for England.

'Go away!' she grated fiercely.

'Emma! I'm sorry that happened,' he said shakily. Astonished by the sincerity in his tone, she searched his face. He seemed very upset. 'I'm sorry,' he repeated helplessly.

Bewildered, she mastered her trembling lip. 'I'd f-forgotten,' she mumbled, thrown completely into confusion by his hand, which was sympathetically stroking her cheek. 'The doll... I should have realised...but...' She couldn't go on. The joy had been too intense, the disappointment too wounding.

He put a comforting hand on hers. 'It was a bad moment for you.' He removed his hand and cupped her chin and she felt more muddled than ever. 'Poor Lexi. I've been blind.'

'Blind?' she repeated, her brain and her voice in a fog.

'To her needs.'

Emma's heart skipped a beat. She looked at him with huge, wondering eyes, her lips parted with breathless hope. Of course Leon didn't care particularly that she'd been hurt. But he did care about Lexi. And maybe he'd see that her daughter truly needed her. It was possible that he'd stop trying to get her on the next flight back to England and would allow the relationship to develop. She had a slim, but welcome chance.

'Leon,' she cried fervently, grabbing his arms in her desperation. 'You want me to give up and go home. But you can't keep us apart. It would be wrong. You can see that, can't you? She wants her mother.'

'Sure. A mother, perhaps. But...*you*?' he said gratingly.

She winced. 'You think I'm a criminal but I'm not. And even if I were,' she added hotly, 'does that make any difference to the fact that Lexi wants a real mother of her own? Not Marina, or Natasa, or any other woman you bring into your life, but *me*! I've only known her for a few hours today but already I can see that she has sensed that something's missing in her life. Let me be part of her world, Leon. She needs me.'

'You're asking too much,' he muttered.

'Not if you really do care about her,' she cried passionately. 'You'd put your own revenge and anger aside and do what's best for her.'

For a long time he contemplated her and she held her breath waiting for his verdict. 'I need time to work out the best way of dealing with this.'

'How long?' she whispered.

'I don't know,' he snapped irritably. 'As long as it takes. I wasn't going to let you near her originally. Part of me wishes I'd stuck to my guns—'

'And the other part?' she asked anxiously, scanning his frowning face.

'Is worrying what damage you'll do to both of us,' he growled.

'Why would I want to hurt my own child? That little mite...' Her words became caught up in her tightened throat. 'Leon, I'll be careful. Sensitive,' she promised desperately.

'You can set the agenda. I'll be her daddy's friend until you say it's time to tell her the truth—'

'It could be a long while.'

'I have the rest of my life,' she replied with heartfelt passion. 'What could be more important?'

'I do believe you mean that,' he muttered. 'I've never known anyone so determined.' He hesitated, his eyes brooding. 'I'll give it some thought. I will do what I consider to be best for Lexi. *Your* wishes don't come into it. And now stop restricting my blood supply.'

She looked down and snatched away her hands from his arms. There were marks where her fingers had been where her nails had dug into his flesh. 'Sorry about that. I got carried away—'

'You always do,' he said, his expression brooding.

Her victory was beginning to sink in. 'I feel very passionately about my daughter. I know you do too.' She slumped, feeling quite drained suddenly.

'It's been an exhausting day for you,' he observed softly.

'I've loved it,' she protested.

'Hmm. Love-hate, I think.'

That was true. But she wouldn't have missed it for the world. She fell silent, summoning up the will to stand and begin the long walk back. Groggily she got to her feet and she gripped the banister as if her life depended on it. Step by step she fumbled her way down the stairs.

There only remained the huge hall to tackle. She eyed it doubtfully but set off, her eyes fixed grimly on the massive wooden door. Behind her she could hear Leon talking to Natasa. And then he'd stridden past and was opening the door for her, an unreadable look on his face.

'See you tomorrow,' she said weakly, before he could suggest an appointment sometime in the future. And she stumbled helter-skelter down the steps outside.

'Wait. I'm going to walk you back.' A torch was flashing along the path ahead, picking out the way for her.

'I can manage,' she snapped, and spoiled her proud independence by tripping over her own feet.

Leon's arms caught her waist and she felt his warm body against her spine and buttocks before she could wrench herself free. He was aroused again. He'd do himself a favour if he hurried back to Natasa, she thought crossly.

'Stubborn woman! You're too tired to see straight,' he rebuked.

'Yes. And not in the mood for company,' she snapped.

Half tearful in her impatience with her irritating tendency to be feeble whenever she needed her strength most, she stumbled again. And this time his arm crooked around her waist and wouldn't be shifted.

'Stop fighting me,' Leon said in an unfairly low and husky tone. 'I can't let you go back on your own in this condition—'

'More than your reputation's worth,' she muttered sourly.

'It would look bad,' he agreed drily, 'if you were found in a state of collapse on my land.'

'I'd rather crawl back on my hands and knees than put you through such shame!' she flung, hot from the pressure of his hip against hers.

'You're unbelievably obstinate,' he said with a sigh. 'One of Lexi's endearing traits. If she wants to finish a task she's set herself, she'll do it come hell or high water.'

Emma raised a weak and fond smile. 'Good on her!'

She considered the trembling muscles in her legs and then the path stretching ahead. It looked daunting.

'Long way, isn't it?' Leon murmured, interpreting her frown correctly.

Her mind might be obstinate but her legs were begging for assistance. She heaved a resigned sigh. 'OK, Leon. You're right. I am shattered and in the absence of a minibus or a Zimmer frame, I suppose you'll have to do.'

'Was it...very difficult for you today?' he asked as they continued.

She sighed. 'Very. You were right. It hurt.'

'But you want to repeat the torture.'

She smiled ruefully, remembering it all. 'Of course. It was wonderful, too. She is adorable. I love her dearly.'

'You found it exhausting being with her.'

And how! Her limbs felt as heavy as lead and she couldn't prevent her body from drooping. 'I'll be fine once I'm fully fit,' she said in a tired voice.

'Toddlers are very demanding—'

'Are you suggesting I'm not up to being with her?' she said flaring.

He squeezed her waist. 'Relax. I'm not trying to score points. I'm saying that I understand. I suggest you have a rest tomorrow. Swim, laze around—'

'You're stalling me. I want to see Lexi,' she cried helplessly.

'I know,' he said soothingly. 'But I need time to think.'

'Can't you do that while I'm around?' she pleaded.

'No. I can't,' he muttered.

'I won't get in the way. I'll play with—'

'Emma,' he interrupted tightly, 'I can't think, I can't concentrate with you there. Accept that and do yourself a favour too, take a break. It was a struggle today, wasn't it? You pushed yourself to keep going but I saw how much of an effort it was towards the end. Do you want to burn yourself out before you've got very far? Does that make sense?'

He was right and she hated him for that. It upset her that she wasn't really well enough to see Lexi every day. A deafening silence fell between them. They trudged on, bruising mint and basil and thyme underfoot. She tried to find her breath but it had run away and her mouth was doing its stupid wobble again.

Leon stopped and gently held her. She stared bleakly at his shirt front. It was a strange blue-white in the darkness and she gazed in mesmerised fascination at the powerful rise and fall of his chest.

'I know you, Emma,' he said softly. 'You are normally full of boundless energy and enthusiasm, just like Lexi. But you're not yourself at the moment and it's obvious that you need to conserve your strength. Rest tomorrow. Sleep all day if you want, what does it matter?'

A sudden breeze played with her hair, whisking it about her face and he gently lifted golden strands away, his warm fingertips brushing her cool skin. She looked up and fell prey to his compelling eyes.

Petrified that she'd make the same mistake twice and inch forwards for a kiss, she tore her glance away and gazed stoically into the velvet night beyond his broad shoulder.

'You...you won't hold it against me?' she said jerkily. 'You won't point out to the courts that I couldn't be bothered to see Lexi, but preferred to laze around—?'

The tightening of his grip stopped her. 'No, Emma.' He seemed to struggle with his thoughts. 'If you must know...I don't want you bursting into tears or breaking up in front of Lexi. That won't do her any good at all. If you carry on driving yourself too hard, you might well lose control. I know your composure is being sorely tested because I have some idea of how you're feeling, being shut out of her life—'

'Yes, I know you do,' she said, remembering his problems with Soula.

His lashes lowered to hide his dark, impassioned eyes and she felt suddenly dizzy with weariness.

'You're swaying,' he said thickly. 'I should have got the car out. Let's get you back.'

They walked hip to hip like lovers, Leon's head bent over hers solicitously, though she knew it was because he was merely worried that she might keel over and have to be carried.

Her arm had found its way around his waist and she allowed it to stay there. For added support, she told herself, but knew that was a lie. She just wanted to sink into his arms and sleep, to wake with him beside her and to gaze at the beautiful angles of his face.

But he was her implacable enemy and would fight tooth and nail to keep her daughter, whatever concessions he granted her now.

The villa was ahead. After today's family fun, it would be silent and lonely in there. Depressed, Emma pushed Leon away.

'Thank you,' she said unhappily. 'Goodnight.'

He continued to walk beside her as she stumbled drunkenly along. 'I must see you to your door—'

'Checking up on me?' she blurted out, too miserable to think what she was saying. She wanted Leon: his sympathy, his body, his respect. And he was off limits. So she'd turn herself against him. 'Do you want to make sure I haven't got an orgy organised?'

'If you have, I hardly think,' he said, sounding gently amused, 'that you'd be up to it.'

'No. I'm sorry I said that,' she muttered, immediately ashamed of herself. She really wasn't cut out to be a bitch. 'You've been kind...gone out of your way to see me home—'

'Here, let me. I don't think you can cope with locks either,' he said, and she realised she'd been trying to put the key in upside down. 'I hadn't realised you were that shattered.'

She leaned against the door jamb, her whole body shaking. 'Lexi doesn't give her heart easily, does she?' she said with a doleful face.

'She takes her time. Weighs people up. Gives them that basilisk stare and waits to see if they run screaming,' he agreed.

'It pained me more than you could ever know,' she said dispiritedly. 'You said you'd put me through hell. Well...' she choked, tears blinding her '...you've succeeded.'

'Emma...'

He'd followed her in. But she'd had enough. She stood in the middle of the room shaking with tension.

'Go!' she said jerkily. 'Just *go*!'

'I...can't,' he said huskily.

'Why?' Emma wailed, wanting him, hating him, muddled, beyond coherent thought.

'I don't know. Or...perhaps I know too well. I—I feel some responsibility for you—'

'Too late!' She hurled the words hysterically, lurching towards the bedroom. 'I needed you years ago,' she said stormily. 'I needed you to believe me when I was accused of fraud. I needed you to tell me we were finished and you were getting engaged...'

It was too much to bear. She choked on her tears and gave up, slamming the bedroom door behind her and jamming a chair against the handle.

Somehow she dragged off her clothes, had a perfunctory wash and crawled into bed. It was only when she turned out the light that she heard the front door close. Leon had left. She burst into tears again.

Leon found it hard to concentrate. He'd slept badly, Emma's forlorn face had firmly stuck on the back of his eyelids, burning into his brain with the force of an indestructible laser image. Even now, at ten in the morning, she was in his eyes, his mind, and his body...

And he didn't even have Lexi to occupy him. Natasa had taken her to town to do 'women's things', 'Tasa had said, and the two of them had run to 'Tasa's car giggling with glee.

Emma's doll had gone too. Leon wasn't sure if he was glad or worried that it accompanied Lexi everywhere, into the bathroom that morning, for breakfast on the terrace, and then—duly coated in 'sun cream' and complete with rucksack just like Lexi—into the car.

His mind darted about like a butterfly. Thinking of golden

hair sweeping briefly, seductively over a softly curved cheek. Of a face tight with desperate longing, arms fidgeting because they couldn't do what they'd been made to do: cuddle a child. And the body…the body! He groaned.

After losing his second e-mail of the day and failing to make sense of a perfectly simple company balance sheet, he leapt irritably from his desk and grabbed some gear for the beach.

He needed an emotional break too. He'd swim till he dropped. And think of nothing, not even tip-tilted lips that needed kissing.

Twenty minutes later he knew it had been a good decision. Lulled by the droning of bees as he strolled through the garden, he let his tense body relax.

A griffon vulture soared overhead. Delicate mauve thistles carpeted the olive grove beyond. A faint breeze stirred the fronds of the date-palms, sending them clacking and as he approached the beach, swallowtail butterflies decorated the garrigue—the low herb undergrowth—like darting jewels.

He stood at the top of the sandy bay to admire its voluptuous sweep. And his pulses quickened to see another voluptuous shape. Emma.

He groaned, knowing he had to go back. And found his legs carrying him inexorably forward. She needed to be alone. To rest and recuperate. So did he—and he wouldn't get any rest with her around. His muscles always knotted up.

Right, that was agreed. They shouldn't be together. The fire was too easily lit in his blood…

But she was there. Alone. And something tugged him inexorably on, ignoring sense and caution.

'I'm surprised to find you down here,' he discovered himself saying quietly.

She sat up on the lounger, visibly flustered. He wasn't too composed either. Unlike yesterday, when she'd worn a one-piece, she was in a small and wonderfully revealing bikini which made the most of her slim body and spectacular curves. Her hands had come to protect her chest, an odd reaction, which had made his gaze linger there longer than wise.

His nails dug into his palms, which helped. He tried to look nonchalant and thought it would help if he sat down on the sunbed beside her.

'Sorry to intrude,' he said with unreal cheerfulness. 'I just fancied a swim in the sea.'

She smiled hesitantly, clearly weighing up his mood and to his surprise he found himself beaming in pleasure. Her smile broadened in response to his inane grin and he realised she was nervous. She was wondering if his verdict was for or against her.

Behind her sunglasses, her eyes were unreadable. He hoped the same applied to his because he was already lusting unmercifully.

'So did I.' Encouraged by his friendly nod, she went on. 'I—I had a long, long sleep and feel a lot better. And I'd…liked it here so much yesterday that…I wanted to spend the day here,' she said haltingly.

'Me too. Do you mind if I stay?'

He frowned. Why had he said that? She might object, in which case—

'How could I? It is your beach, after all.' She eyed him uncertainly. 'But I'll go if you're going to growl at me. I need a restful day for a change.'

'I won't growl,' he promised, managing to hold back a sigh of relief. 'I'm looking for an uncomplicated few hours, schlepping out. Deal?'

She grinned back at him and seemed delighted. 'Deal.'

Her head tipped back to enjoy the sun, the action raising the contours of her breasts. Leon tried not to notice his racing pulses, and studiously averted his gaze and fixed it sternly on the dazzling sea.

'I'm glad you feel better,' he ventured to say. And wondered why he felt that way and how banal his conversation was going to get.

'I really needed a break. I've been under a great strain for a long time,' she said quietly.

'I can imagine.'

Again, a pang of pity—and his low, caring voice must have conveyed that pity to her. But she'd brought her troubles on herself. He had to remember that.

And yet he knew he couldn't help feeling great sympathy for her. Lexi was her baby. And a stranger. He frowned, washed by pain on her behalf.

She sighed, the pleasure of that outrush of breath attracting his attention. Her eyes were closed in contentment, the sun gleaming on her pale gold skin. He felt his throat go dry.

'Where's Lexi?' she murmured.

He gave a joking groan. 'Buying up every pink dress in Zakynthos with Natasa.'

He checked himself. She'd winced and he realised he'd put his foot in it. It must hurt her to have some other woman doing things with her daughter.

'She...she's fond of Lexi,' Emma observed, turning her head to study him closely. 'Does...does Lexi ever call her Mama?'

It was his turn to wince. More and more he was beginning to realise that he couldn't exclude Emma from Lexi's life. But the implications of changing tack were alarming.

'Only once.'

'Once is enough, Leon!'

He looked deep into her startlingly blue eyes. 'I know. It upset Natasa. She made sure that Lexi knew that she wasn't in the running for that position.' From the anxious look on Emma's face, the relationship needed clarifying. And perhaps a little more than that. 'My sister-in-law,' he explained, 'adores children.'

'Sister-in-law!' It seemed the light had dawned. 'She's Marina's sister?'

He nodded and could see her brain turning over the information. 'Her husband died six months ago from cancer. For some reason she's convinced she'll never marry again and have babies of her own. Which is ridiculous, of course, but it gives her great happiness to spend time with Lexi. And I want 'Tasa to be happy. She nursed her husband devotedly and I admire her, and wish her well.'

'A diamond among women. Poor Natasa! It must have been terrible for her to lose her husband at such a young age. All her dreams, her plans for the future...' Her voice petered out.

Natasa's story seemed to have touched a chord with Emma. He saw that she was struggling with a profound sympathy, a kind of horror that went far beyond any normal reaction.

'Emma?' He touched her arm and she jumped.

'I—I was thinking. Was it quick?' she asked, her face pale.

'Her husband's death? Yes, mercifully so.' It seemed that she waited to hear more. 'They both came to stay with me. It helped her to cope. It meant she could forget normal household activities and concentrate on being with her husband. We knew it was terminal.'

'Difficult for you all,' she observed, her expression full of concern.

There was something about her that invited his confidences. He'd never spoken about Natasa to anyone outside the immediate family. And even to them he'd never revealed his own feelings. But suddenly he felt a need to open up.

'I think the worst part for me was when I heard her crying all alone at night,' he said quietly. 'I could do so much to help her, but there were some things she had to face on her own. That was hard for me to accept. I wanted to take away her anguish completely.'

'You can't,' Emma said. 'People have to go through that grieving process. She was mourning for her husband and herself. It's a mistake to think you can leap-frog misery. It has to be faced, and then it's been dealt with—and you're the stronger for it. You did all the right things, Leon.'

'Did I?' He wasn't sure.

'You gave her support when she needed it. She cares very deeply for you—'

'And I for her.' Without her, he didn't know what he would have done. She had been—and would be—his lifeline.

Emma's white teeth snagged at her lower lip. 'So…you're helping her to adjust. You're making her feel useful and she's fussing over you and Lexi like…like…a mother hen,' she finished jerkily.

He wasn't sure why she was on edge. Perhaps because she believed Natasa was taking over her role. Anxious to put Emma straight, he took her hand in his to capture her attention.

'Natasa will never be Lexi's surrogate mother,' he said gently. Her enormous eyes remained fixed on his hopefully and he knew he'd hit on the answer to her fears. 'And the reason she's here is that when her husband died she asked if she could help run the house. She needed to be with family for a while and needed an excuse to stay without feeling she was a parasite. My housekeeper was ready to retire, so it seemed a good arrangement.'

Emma frowned at their interlocked fingers. 'Wasn't there gossip, with you both living in the same house?'

'Not with Marina there too, and Soula. Natasa is devoted to her sister and everyone knows we are just an extended family. It's not an uncommon arrangement.'

'Poor Natasa,' she said again. 'I hope she finds happiness one day.'

Happiness. There were several levels of it. He was content enough. But once he had known a happiness that had filled every cell in his body with the joy of living. Would that rapture ever be part of him again?

'I think I'll go for a swim,' she muttered.

He watched her walking thoughtfully to the water's edge.

In the old days she would have turned a cartwheel or two in sheer exuberance, but she was different now. Sometimes the old impetuosity surfaced, but mostly she was sad and subdued. He wanted to change that, to see her laugh more frequently.

After a decent interval, he hauled off his T-shirt and ran into the sea, plunging his hot and tense body into the cool turquoise water. It was a while before he paused in his ferocious crawl and began to swim for pleasure. Eventually he turned on his back and floated, staring up at the bright blue sky. When he struck out for shore, he saw her towelling herself dry on the beach.

Decision time. He sat on the edge of the water, thinking of the emotional mess that Soula was in and how his calm, gentle influence had been worse than useless and soon he'd have to accept that and leave Marina and Soula to their own devices.

It hurt to admit it, but Emma was right. Lexi would probably be more balanced if she knew her biological mother. He watched the sea lapping over his feet. There were some things you couldn't stop. Tides and love being two of those.

But the danger for Lexi if he agreed—for his peace of mind! Perhaps, he thought, as the water swirled in a rush around his entire body, he could cope with the prospect of Emma's access visits. All he had to do was to make sure that she was never alone with Lex—not now, or any time in the future.

Aware that he was making a momentous about-turn, he jumped up and walked quickly to where Emma was sitting, her honey-gold body bolt upright in the lounger.

'You've decided! You'll let me stay and befriend Lexi!' she cried eagerly, when he was still a yard or so away.

His eyes widened in stark surprise. 'How the devil did you know?'

'I read you,' she cried happily.

'*Read* me?'

'The way you sat there, thinking—and your body language... Besides, I felt sure you'd do the right thing.'

He grunted and sat on the edge of his lounger facing her. 'Don't make me regret it, Emma,' he warned. 'If you harm that child—'

'I wouldn't!' she cried with elation, swinging her legs around to mirror his pose. 'Lexi's welfare comes first, I promise you that,' she said softly. 'Thank you for giving me this chance.'

'It's for Lexi, not you.'

Or was it? He didn't know any more, only that he felt as if a burden had been lifted from his shoulders. He'd see her often. Feed his eyes on her. Get to know her. Spirals of pleasure rippled through him, shortening his breath. Madness.

'That's why I felt sure you must agree,' she said happily.

'You hit a raw nerve.'

'Did I? Good!' she exulted.

'I don't want Lexi confused,' he continued, trying to quieten his own leaping nerves. But he couldn't get enough of her ecstatic face and her joy was lifting his soul. She seemed to glow with life. And he wanted to kiss her till she couldn't draw breath. 'We do this gradually. Be guided by me.'

'Yes, Leon,' she agreed with a laugh. 'Oh, I'm so happy!'

She jumped up, her face rapturous. And, impulsive as ever, she bent forward and kissed both his cheeks. Fatally, he had imprisoned her face between his hands before he knew what he was doing. And their mouths met, first clumsily, then fiercely as Emma's euphoria carried her beyond the realms of caution.

Then she pushed at his shoulders. Reluctantly he let a gap form between their lips and his hot eyes met her troubled blue ones.

'I can't believe I just did that!' she exclaimed, her hand in front of her soft mouth.

Ditto. He managed a casual grin. 'You always did need to let off steam.'

Scarlet with embarrassment, she nodded, seizing on his excuse with alacrity. 'That's it! And I will!' she cried, leaping up.

And to his delight, she ran along the firm sand by the lapping waves, turning a series of perfect cartwheels.

CHAPTER EIGHT

'I THOUGHT we'd feed the animals,' Leon said casually the next morning, when he and Lexi arrived at her villa, as they'd arranged.

'Animals?' Emma asked, smiling broadly to see Lexi jumping up and down excitedly.

'Chittens,' Lexi explained loftily, holding out a soggy and distorted lump of bread. It had clearly been squeezed fiercely in her little hand for some while and Emma's eyes softened with amused affection.

'Chickens and turkeys, goats, sheep and geese,' Leon said indulgently. 'Come on. I'll show you. Lexi saved that from breakfast, didn't you, sweetheart?' He repeated that in Greek and she nodded so vigorously that her scrunchie fell out of her silky hair.

'Here. I can do it,' Emma offered eagerly.

But Lexi pulled away, glaring at Emma from under her lowered brows with an expression so like Leon's that it caught at her throat. And she tried not to mind the rejection. It was early days yet. But, despite her reasoning, it still hurt.

'Hold the scrunchie for me, will you Emma?' Leon asked casually. He put down his own bag of stale bread, scooped up Lexi's curls into his hand and gave them an admirably fashionable twist.

She was grateful to him for involving her. The smile she bestowed on him was pure gold and Leon responded with a conspiratorial wink as he fixed the hair problem with a deftness born of long practice.

'The animals belong to the caretaker,' Leon explained, when they were eventually on their way—a tickle, a cuddle

120

and a ride on his shoulders later. 'He rang to say that the turkeys had chicks so I thought Lex might like to see them.'

The smallholding lay beyond a field of low currant vines which marched across the red, rich soil in military ranks. With Lexi's legs wrapped suffocatingly around his neck, his head reluctantly doubling as a drum for her small hands, Leon led the way beneath a bower of wild honeysuckle to a lemon grove, seemingly alive with cheeping grey chicks.

'There they are,' he cried, lowering Lexi to the ground.

'Chittens!' Lexi cried with joy, and hurtled after them.

'She's got my finesse,' Emma said ruefully, seeing the turkey chicks scatter in alarm as the blonde bombshell approached. 'Delicate as a stampeding bull.'

'Enthusiasm, and it's wonderful,' Leon corrected with a grin. He scraped a hand through his mussed hair.

'So long as you're not a chitten.' She giggled.

Leon laughed and ran to catch Lexi's hand and to show her how to win the confidence of the chicks. With great patience he taught her to throw her bread as far as possible at first and then increasingly closer and closer.

However, Lexi's aim wasn't too good and Emma and Leon kept chuckling as one or two of the tiny chicks narrowly missed concussion from the heavy lumps.

'Hello, chittens!' Lexi whispered, awed, as they cheeped with enthusiastic recklessness around her feet.

'Chicks.'

'Chits.'

'Stand very still, sweetheart,' he said lovingly, and Lexi turned into a rigid statue, only her fingers daring to move. Which made her aim even worse.

Leon gave Emma some bread and, with it, a sideways grin. He's wonderful, she thought, admiring his patience with her over-eager daughter. And she tried hard to understand his slow and careful Greek when they went to dispense grain for the chickens and to feed the other animals in the enclosure.

Then, by a clump of cornflowers, something caught her eye and she bent down to see what it was.

'Look!' she cried, her voice hushed in pleasure. 'I've found an egg.' It was freshly laid. She crouched down and smiled at Lexi. 'Hold out your hand,' she said in English, showing her what she meant.

A small and sticky palm was hesitantly extended and Emma gently slid the egg into it. The look on her daughter's face made her heart turn over.

'It's warm!' Lexi squeaked.

'Gently,' Leon warned, his voice low and soft. 'It will break easily.'

'Oh, oh, oh!' Lexi whispered, magnificently reining in her obvious desire to leap about in glee.

'For your breakfast,' Emma suggested, wishing she could be there.

Her daughter beamed at her, the blue eyes searingly bright. 'Yes. Thank-you-very-much.'

'My pleasure,' Emma whispered happily and her moist eyes met Leon's.

A searing flash of longing went through her and she turned away hastily. For a split second she had yearned for the impossible. That she and Leon and Lexi would be feeding chittens and finding eggs and loving one another for the rest of their lives.

But he despised her and believed she had not only defrauded innocent people, but had been the indirect cause of his brother's death. And, though he might not be averse to kissing her, he certainly wouldn't welcome her freely into his highly protected home.

The dream had been too welcome, the reality harsh. Unless she altered her plans radically, she would be taking her daughter away from all this. Her eyes widened. How could she do that to her child? This paradise...

She swallowed. It was her own fault. Leon had warned her that she'd realise Lexi's future lay here—and that the knowledge would be painful to accept. And she'd recklessly brushed aside his caution, seeing it as a threat. But perhaps he'd been right. Doubts gnawed at her, spoiling the happy moment and her stomach felt suddenly hollow.

'We're going back to Emma's villa now. The animals are all breaded-out.' Leon's voice was warm and gentle, close to her ear.

She shivered and tried to perk up. 'For a swim?' she suggested unsteadily.

Lexi let out a whoop and charged off. Leon threw Emma a grin and ran after her. She heard her daughter wailing—presumably she'd fallen over—and Leon's soothing murmur, a childish giggle, and his deep laugh. How easily a child's distress could be smoothed over.

I want him, she thought. And not just physically. Someone to soothe her hurt, to be there when she needed him. A shoulder to lean on and a friend to share her day, her moments of joy.

Emma stifled those thoughts at birth. Life wasn't that forgiving and Leon certainly wouldn't be.

Later that afternoon, after exhausting games in the pool, Lexi fell fast asleep. Tenderly Leon placed her daughter's limp form on a lounger beneath a walnut tree and joined Emma by the poolside where she sat dangling her legs in the warm water.

'She liked the egg,' he said, easing himself down to the tiled edge.

She smiled. 'Almost as good as the crown jewels.'

'Better. She's fascinated by nature. I'm up all hours of the night trying to keep a few steps ahead of her. I'm OK identifying beetles, but not too hot on finches,' he said ruefully.

'What about bees that look like Zeppelins?' she squealed, as she ducked away from the attentions of a huge insect with iridescent wings. 'Crikey. It's got a buzz that sounds like a chain-saw!'

'Keep still. It won't harm you,' Leon advised, laughing.

The giant bee proved him a liar by doing a circuit of her head, clearly preparing to dive-bomb her and then line up for an emergency landing.

'Help!' She grabbed frantically at Leon.

'I...ooooohaargh! What—?'

He overbalanced and they both toppled into the water, coming up spluttering and laughing. The mock menace on his face made her squeal and she struck out for the steps at the far end of the pool.

Of course he caught her. Emma shrieked when he grabbed her and then became aware of someone else shouting. Still clasped in his firm grip, she jerked her head around to discover a tight-lipped Marina standing on the edge of the pool, clad in a black leather basque and a pelmet skirt, and with her hands on her hips in an attitude of frosty disapproval.

Surprisingly, Leon kept his hands on her waist. 'Hello, Marina. This is Emma—' he began courteously.

'Instead of fooling around with the criminal classes,' Marina snapped nastily, 'how about paying attention to your niece?'

From the increased pressure on her waist, and the clenching of Leon's teeth, Emma expected him to put Marina in her place with a few well-chosen epithets. Instead, he merely said, 'Lexi's asleep.'

There was a splash. Emma jerked her head around and realised that a child of five or six years of age in a pink party dress and with ribbons everywhere conceivable—Soula, without question—was calmly and maliciously throwing objects into the pool. A chair. Her sunglasses. Emma gasped. A towel—

Leon launched himself across the pool in a whoosh of water and hauled himself out.

'Soula, for heaven's sake!' he rebuked.

The little girl screamed and ran away from him, pushing

whatever she could find into the pool as she went. Two mugs, a plate, an orange and Lexi's jelly shoes.

'Now look what you've done!' screeched Marina.

'Soula,' Leon said quietly, restraining his temper with difficulty as a small teak table hit the water, 'please don't do that—'

'Don't come near me!' Soula shouted, stamping her feet. 'Mummee! *Mummee!*'

Emma was horrified by the extraordinary vehemence of Soula's appeal to her mother. The little girl flung herself at her mother's knees and was immediately soothed.

Marina and Leon stared at one another: she spitting fire and hatred, he—oh, thought Emma, her heart going out to him—he was hurt and frustrated with a tortured expression on his face. Sadly she clambered out of the pool, wondering what to do and afraid that Lexi would wake even though Leon had said she slept the sleep of the dead. She headed for her daughter just as Leon hissed, 'Take Lexi in!'

Hastily Emma scooped up the floppy little body, holding it close to her. My child, she thought shakily. In my arms at last but for the most awful reason.

Unsteady on her feet and nervous of her bundle, she climbed the steps with great care up to the villa, then sat in the nearest chair with her, cradling her close.

My baby, my baby, her heart was saying as she gazed down on the sleep-soft face. Oh, my darling baby! She kissed Lexi's head, feeling guilty. It was as if she was violating her daughter's rights. She gulped and restrained her urge to squeeze Lexi tight and kiss every inch of the sweet face.

When she looked up to the scene outside, she saw that Leon was standing over Soula, his hands on his hips.

'Soula, you can't go around doing that!' he said in a rasping voice.

'She's upset because you forgot Lexi was going to Maria's party,' Marina yelled. 'We had to waste time coming here and she'll have missed the clown—'

'I said Lex wouldn't be going,' he replied. 'She didn't seem bothered. Her mother is here—'

Emma looked down sharply. Lexi had given a small sigh. Stealthily, trying not to disturb the sleeping child, she rose from the chair, intending to move back out of earshot. She held her breath and froze. Lexi's eyes opened—and then closed again.

'But you promised,' shouted Marina as Emma cautiously moved further into the open-plan room. 'You can't break that promise.'

Faintly she heard Leon's groan and she paused, straining her ears to listen to his reply. 'That was a week ago, before Emma came—'

'You said you were going to fling the little cow out on her ear!'

Lexi's eyes snapped open. She registered Emma's face, and burst into tears.

'Hush, sweetheart,' Emma murmured, but there was no response from the stiff little body. 'It's OK. It's me.'

She longed desperately to say, It's Mummy. Despite all her attempts she couldn't comfort Lexi. Almost in tears herself, she tried everything she could to soothe the struggling, wriggling and weeping child, but to no avail. And that upset her desperately.

And then Leon was there, taking Lexi from her and holding her sobbing daughter tight, wrapping his big arms around her.

'She didn't hear anything, honestly,' Emma wailed in agitation. 'She just opened her eyes and cried—'

'It's OK, Emma. She was startled.'

Gradually Lexi's sobs lessened as his reassuring voice murmured softly in her small ear.

Startled. By the sight of her own mother. She let out a moan.

Leon was kissing the small, damp face, making a game of capturing the tears with his mouth and smacking his lips noisily. When he pretended to eat her nose and ears and declared them tasty too, she dissolved into giggles, her tears forgotten.

So easy, thought Emma sadly. If only she could comfort her own child. But she wasn't loved. She was a stranger.

Oh, God! she thought, wrapping her arms tightly around her pain-slashed body. I've lost my child. Will I ever get her back?

'The party—' Marina had appeared at the back door.

He let Lexi down to the floor. 'I'll ask her,' he said with apparent calm. But his hands were clenched into fists.

Emma's eyes flashed. She wasn't letting her daughter go off with a mad clothes-horse and her destructive child.

'Leon,' she said grimly, 'a word.'

He took one look at her and seemed to know what was in her mind.

'Natasa is driving,' he said quietly. 'She'll be responsible for Lexi.'

'But—'

'Trust me. Would I put her in an unsuitable situation?'

'N-no—'

'It's none of her business!' Marina snapped.

'She's Lexi's m-o-t-h-e-r,' he said, spelling the word carefully. 'She has every right to be concerned for her daughter's welfare.'

His amiable tone was carefully monitored for Lexi's benefit and Emma detected steel in his eyes when he looked at his ex-wife.

Marina's mouth looked dangerous, ready to spit venom. Emma braced herself, fearful for what Lexi might hear.

'Do you think so? That woman killed your brother!' Marina flung the words, fast and furious. 'Have you *forgotten*—?'

As Emma gasped, Leon crossed the floor in a flash. 'Don't say another word,' he murmured pleasantly. 'Or I'll be tempted to violence. Let me have Lex's party dress. Go and wait in the car. She'll be out in a few moments if she's coming. You've gone too far this time, Marina. We'll talk when you get back.'

Aghast, Emma sank into a chair and stared blankly into space. She'd been so wrapped up in her own problems that she hadn't thought of things from his point of view—however wrong that view might be.

How could a man *like* a woman he thought had been responsible for his brother's death, let alone feel fond of her? And his approval and respect was what she longed for—like Natasa. But there was no evidence to prove her innocent. So he'd always blame her. She groaned.

'I don't want her to go!' Emma whispered in panic when she and Leon were alone again. Fortunately Lexi had become engrossed in playing with her doll.

'I do,' he said firmly. 'There are things I have to say to you immediately—and I need time to do so.'

'But you said I could be with Lex—'

'I did. That was before the scene out there really developed—'

'Scene? It was more like Armageddon!'

'You're exaggerating, Emma,' he said gently.

'Not where Lexi is concerned.'

'It needs explaining. The party is a sleepover. Natasa will watch over her. She keeps a tight rein on her sister and Soula. And Marina doesn't shout at Lexi. Only me.'

'And Soula?' Emma's hands had tightened into fists, ready to defend her child.

'Soula isn't interested in anyone other than herself,' he said bleakly.

'Leon—' she cried, aghast that a father should feel so badly about his child.

'Give me time. I'll explain.'

And he talked gently to Lexi, dangling the pretty baby-blue dress—far more attractive than Soula's—as a lure and soon he had persuaded Lexi into its soft folds, his tone eager and excited as he spoke of the delights ahead.

But when they'd waved goodbye, his cheerful expression was wiped from his face as if a giant hand had erased it. With a hard expulsion of air from his lungs, he sat down heavily on the sofa and, through the open door at the far end of the room, he gloomily surveyed the debris floating in the pool.

Emma ignored it. He needed her more. 'Leon, don't worry,' she said gently, sitting beside him and tentatively stroking his shoulder. 'Lexi didn't hear anything she shouldn't, I'm positive. It...it was just me who made her cry.'

'But she *could* have heard. So far she hasn't, but...' He sucked in a long breath. 'And now you're thinking that this isn't paradise after all,' he muttered bitterly. 'And you'd be right.'

He looked at her, his eyes bleak and infinitely pained and in an instinctive action she took his head in her hands and laid it on her breast, enfolding him in her arms and rocking him.

The scene she'd witnessed had been appalling. Not the kind of thing to risk exposing a child to. She had ammunition, she thought sadly, to put before the courts. And it gave her no pleasure.

'I don't understand,' she said, stroking his dark, shining hair. A lump came into her throat. 'Why, if you and Marina hate the sight of each other, do you let her stay with you? You're divorced. You don't have to make each other's lives hell.'

He drew away a little and heaved such a despairing sigh that she felt like cuddling him and kissing him better.

'Leon,' she whispered, afraid that she cared too much. 'Tell me,' she begged. 'I want to help if I can.'

His arm came to rest around her shoulders and he pulled her close. 'Hold me,' he said simply. 'That helps.'

With concern in every fibre of her being, she did as he

asked. And soon, when his breathing had settled to a more normal rate, she ventured again.

'Marina. Soula.'

She bit her lip, worrying that the child would be a terrible influence on little Lexi. And the rows must be distressing, if that was a sample. Her eyes widened as she remembered something.

'When you were visiting me in prison, Marina was looking after Lexi!' she said in horror.

'Not exactly,' he replied. 'It was Natasa who took charge. But if I'd said Marina's sister-in-law was caring for your daughter, you would have gone ballistic. Look, let's clear the pool then get dressed and make a cup of tea,' he said shakily. 'And I'll tell you everything.'

In silence he walked out and dived into the pool, lifting the objects out. Emma and he then sluiced them under the pool shower and dried some, leaving the sun to dry the others.

Then they went back inside. Alarmed by his brooding lethargy, she watched him walk slowly up the stairs to the bedroom where he'd left his clothes. His steps slowed overhead and she found herself listening out for him anxiously as she hurried to her own bedroom, showered and scrambled into a simple scoop-neck T-shirt and denim button-through skirt, dragging a quick brush through her hair.

Rushing out, she put just a little water in the kettle and grabbed a couple of mugs and two teabags, opting for speed over elegance. The tea was made by the time he came down, steam coiling up from the mugs which she'd placed on the low marble table in front of the sofa.

She watched his slow progress down the stairs and her heart missed a beat. Edible as ever in the mint green shirt and stone chinos, he had a vague, distracted air which wasn't like him at all.

'Sit down,' she said taking charge. She occupied one end of the sofa and intended him to feel he could reach out for whatever comfort he needed so she patted the space beside her. 'I want to know it all.'

When he came over it seemed natural that he should pull her against him again so they were curled up together, her head on his chest, her arm flung loosely around his waist.

'It goes way back,' he began softly. 'You accused me of abandoning you when I got engaged. It wasn't that simple.'

'No?'

To her surprise he kissed the top of her head and she stopped breathing for a moment. He turned her till they were gazing into one another's eyes. He smiled, and said huskily and with infinite sadness, 'I did love you.'

Her breath knifed in sharply, in small shuddering gasps. Then she gulped.

'Then...why did you break my heart?' she asked, quite bewildered.

His finger traced her hairline. Her eyes flickered shut, long lashes veiling the pained blue beneath.

'Duty,' he replied harshly.

'Leon—'

His mouth found hers, softened in a gentle kiss that made her moan—and then was gone.

'We'd been out to that students' charity run, remember? We made love in my digs and arranged to meet the next day. You were wearing a bright blue shirt and jeans and you had your hair up, as you did just now when you were swimming.'

She couldn't believe he'd remembered. 'Then...we said goodnight,' she said jerkily.

Leon tensed. 'And later that same night, I had a call from my father. He was, to my surprise, in England. He'd come over with members of the Christofides family. We had been linked in business partnership with them for several generations,' he explained. 'Father sounded upset. We arranged a breakfast meeting for seven o'clock in his hotel.'

Emma listened to the low, tortured tones with apprehension. She had never known Leon so subdued.

'It was an arranged marriage, wasn't it? A dynastic affair—'

'Not exactly,' he replied slowly. 'The problem was that Marina, who's the only daughter and heiress of Anton Christofides—my father's dearest friend—was in trouble.'

Emma's head shifted imperceptibly so that she was looking up at him. She knew what trouble meant.

'Pregnant?' she asked sharply. 'By *you*?'

'No, no, Emma.' He squeezed her reassuringly and she subsided, her heart pounding. 'By a tourist.' Bitterness invaded his tone.

'What? Are you saying…Soula isn't your child?' she squeaked.

'Exactly,' he muttered. 'Marina was only just seventeen and quite a handful. Very wilful and spoiled rotten. Her father was out of his mind. The shame…'

'They…' She tensed and so did he, warily watching the look of sheer horror that was spreading across her face. 'They made you marry Marina to cover up what had happened?' she cried in outrage. 'And you agreed? How could you, Leon? How could you?' She battered her fists against his chest in frustration and he caught her wrists in self-defence, wrestling with her. 'It's gross,' she complained. 'You loved me. I loved you.' Wriggling, she tried to escape him but he wrapped his legs around her body and held her fast. 'Let me go!' she sobbed. 'I can't believe you could do such a thing. *Let—me—go!*'

He was silent. Hot-faced and furious, she squirmed till her T-shirt was rucked up and in danger of revealing her naked breasts beneath.

'You're a rat! You ruined my life for the sake of a—a spoiled female who'd—'

Leon's mouth enclosed hers. For a few moments she fought its pressure, her head whirling at the wonderful sense of liquidity in her bones. And then she began to allow the pleasure to flow through her, helpless to resist its insistent beat.

'Emma.' He grated her name urgently against her lips, dropping kisses there which were so delicate and tantalising that she stupidly flung her arm around his neck and snaked her body against his. 'You must let me explain.'

'Wait a minute! You're lying!' She raged, coming to her senses. She'd remembered something. 'It wasn't a sudden surprise to you at all. I was there. I saw the banner, the menu—'

'They'd been done here, on the island, as an urgent order before everyone left. They were so sure I'd agree.'

Emma saw that Leon's eyes were still drugged with desire and she battled with her hunger and her love. Feeling like that was madness. He'd all but destroyed her with his sense of duty. Had sent her hurtling into Taki's arms. And Taki's ruthless domination. Two years in jail. *The loss of her child.*

What had she been thinking of?

Cold, her eyes shimmering with anger, she said jerkily through clenched teeth, 'OK. Make your excuses. But make them good, Leon—because I'm close enough to ruin your chances of fatherhood for ever.'

CHAPTER NINE

JUDGING by her glittering rage, Leon thought tautly, she could well carry out her threat. He took the precaution of removing his hands from the sweet firmness of her back and waist and, in an effort to protect himself, he hauled her up a little. In doing so, she ended up straddling his pelvis.

It was a mistake. She shuddered throughout her body and as he felt her deep heat seep into him he momentarily lost the plot. She was throbbing. And so was he.

They stared, appalled, at one another. A tornado seemed to be filling his head, ripping out whatever brains and conscious thought he'd had in there, to leave just sense and sensation.

He muttered a curse and found his place in the story by sheer dogged effort of will. She would understand even if he had to force every word down her throat. No one was going to call him a rat. He'd acted as honourably as he could. A tiny little voice told him that, from Emma's point of view, that could never be so.

'Dammit, Emma!' he snapped, savage in his frustration for sex and for her understanding. 'You weren't there. You didn't know what it was like.'

'Enlighten me,' she said flaring, her chest heaving.

The movement of her untrammelled breasts, hard-tipped and hovering far too close to his hands, combined with the pooling heat between them, almost sabotaged his mind again.

Where the hell was he? He shut his eyes tightly and it came to him and when he opened them again he was only briefly diverted by the puffy little breaths she was taking through her parted lips.

134

She thought the worst of him. And that was infinitely unjust.

'Do you think I didn't argue?' he demanded roughly. 'That I didn't tell them I was in love? I was reminded of my *duty*.' He spat the word out, hating it and what it had done to his life. 'Both my family and hers put pressure on me. They were depending on me—I was the only person who could help. There *was* no one else, I realised that immediately. Understand my dilemma!' he demanded urgently. 'These were people I was close to. They were turning to me to solve a desperate situation. I've always admired and respected Anton Christofides. He's my godfather—and in my country that role creates a special bond between the child and godparent. He's been like a second father to me. I care about him deeply. And there he was—this confident, assured and highly respected man—looking utterly distraught, despairing even, and begging me to save his daughter from dishonour.'

He raked his hand through his hair, bleakly remembering the chilling sense of inevitability as he'd tried to come up with any other solution than the one that had been proposed.

'It was a nightmare,' he muttered. 'All the time I could hear Marina sobbing her heart out in the other room. She was virtually a child, however wilful, Emma! And then they brought her out to persuade me. She flung herself at me and pleaded with me to agree. I've never known anyone so hysterical. She had a razor in her hand and I wasn't sure if she was going to slit her own wrists or mine! Do you know what that's like? To have someone's life depend on you? Should I have turned my back?' he cried passionately. 'At the very least I would have lost my father's respect—the father I loved and honoured above all men. I would have lost my extended family, Emma, and destroyed people I loved. But, far worse than that, Marina might have carried out her threat to kill herself...'

He broke off, choking as the past heaved back in graphic clarity: the despair, anger, pity... 'And the baby, Emma,' he said, choking on the words. 'She swore she'd have an abortion if I didn't marry her.' His mouth twisted at the horror of it. 'I couldn't bear that. I couldn't be responsible for the death of her child.'

Emma was quiet now, her eyes full of sympathy. She curled up against him again, reaching up to stroke his forehead. He realised it had been creased in a worried frown. But this meant so much to him. For years he'd wanted to clear the air.

'You could have told me all this at the time,' she said grumpily.

'No, that wouldn't have worked. If I had seen you, I would never have gone through with it. When I knew I had to agree, for Marina and her unborn baby's sake, I had to block you out of my life. It was better that you should hate me. It meant I wouldn't be tempted to change my mind. I had to believe that I could come to love her and her child,' he said passionately.

'Did you?' she asked in a small voice.

'No—though I tried. Oh, I loved Soula at first but Marina was always difficult. And my wife in name only.'

His eyes grew bleak. The days had been a nightmare, tiptoeing about the hysterical Marina, ducking flying objects and listening to her screeching over some trifle. A lost lipstick, a mislaid flight ticket... God! He'd never known such people existed.

'Leon...?' Emma touched his face, her eyes full of questions.

He blanked out the hell of those years and tried to sound dispassionate.

'I'm the head of the family. That's what I must do.'

'Your duty.' There was a pause as they both considered that. 'But,' she said breathily, sending shivers of air across his jaw, 'you're not exactly thrilled with the situation.'

'No,' he admitted. 'It's hell. So far Lexi hasn't been affected—Marina and Soula keep to themselves most of the time and I'm merely a wallet on legs. But...God, I don't know what to do for the best sometimes,' he finished moodily. 'I've made a mess of things. I should have left them to their own devices and not confused Soula with my house rules—but it's hard, seeing a child being brought up with widely differing values to yours.'

'What do you think Marina wants in life?' she asked.

'Money,' he answered without hesitation.

'Love, Leon,' she corrected. 'We all need love.'

He was silent, his heart in total agreement. And then said quietly, 'I couldn't give that to her. A roof over her head and financial security, yes, courtesy, sympathy, time...but not love.'

Emma saw the link. She'd had none to give to Taki, because she'd squandered it on Leon. And the marriage had foundered.

'I think you should let go,' she mused. 'All the time you're around, it's not giving Marina a chance to strike out and find her soul mate. It isn't any of your business how she brings up her child, and you seem to be the catalyst for their anger. As far as prospective boyfriends for Marina are concerned, you'd put anyone off,' she said bluntly, omitting to explain that men would feel intimidated because he was so charismatic.

'That's exactly what I've decided. I'm talking to Marina in the morning. I'm going to suggest she talks to her father about living with him again. She's visited him a couple of times and I think he and his new wife are happier to have her around, especially if Natasa lives there too. Marina's calmer when Natasa is around. I'll see what they all think. Trouble is, I'd lose a housekeeper.' He rubbed his chin reflectively. 'The caretaker's wife might help out there. Donika's working on the land at the moment. She's always asking me to find her an indoor job. I'll ask her. I'm sure she'd jump at the chance.'

It seemed settled. 'You'll miss Natasa.'

He smiled and her jealousy unfurled its claws. 'I'll miss her biscuits but my waistline will be reprieved,' he said, smiling wanly at his little joke. 'But, yes, I'd miss her.'

'She'll be able to visit,' Emma said, finding her generosity hard to believe.

He said nothing but stroked her hair absently, as if his thoughts were far away. Emma reflected that Marina's fling had not only ruined her own life, but many lives. Leon had tried to do what was right—and in doing so had destroyed his own happiness. She felt very sad. They might have been married now with children of their own.

'Oh, Leon,' she whispered jerkily.

She felt the air between them quiver and lifted her head to judge his expression. His lips had parted, his teeth shining white in the darkness of his face. The drowsy, sultry expression in his eyes served as a warning but she couldn't—wouldn't—heed it.

This was the man she'd loved and lost, the man she'd respected and had adored with every last breath in her body. And he was still that same man. He'd surrendered his own happiness for the sake of a frightened teenager and her unborn child. And now he was hurting and she wanted to ease his pain, to wipe it out as if it had never been and to make his heart whole again.

She smiled at him hazily. Everything had changed. He wasn't heartless—far from it—and she still loved him. Terribly, recklessly, profoundly.

For a brief, wonderful moment, her own heart opened like a flower. And then it closed up again when she realised that she had to protect herself. Her eyes became dull. He might have loved her once—and still lusted after her—but he had a devastatingly low opinion of her.

'Emma,' he murmured seductively.

'Tea,' she said jerkily. 'Getting cold.'

'To hell with the tea.'

'This doesn't change anything,' she said frantically.

'Doesn't it?' His eyes glittered.

'No.' She bit her lip, steeling herself to ignore the mesmeric stroking of his hands as they moved up and down her arms, and the hot message in his liquid eyes. Needing to escape, she wriggled in his grip and found herself being pushed back.

He was kissing her, ignoring her moans of protest, driving his mouth into hers till it throbbed, one hand supporting her spine and crushing her against him, the other running up and down her bare leg which had somehow wound itself wantonly across his thigh.

How had it done that? she wondered. It was almost as if it wanted to encourage him. Appalled, she wrenched her mouth from his and said the first thing that came into her mind.

'I need to ring John.'

He scowled. 'Later.'

'No, please, Leon—'

'Why the desperation?' He bit the words out. 'Won't I do?'

'It's not that—'

'What then?' he challenged. 'If you're so free with your favours—'

'You brute!' she said choking with incredulity, managing to pull herself back a little. Her chest heaved in anger, and her temper was made worse by the miserable sense of disappointment and sexual loss rushing through her shaking body. 'You never believe me. In your eyes I'm a criminal with no morals at all—'

'Right.'

'And I leap into bed with anyone I fancy—'

'Yes!' he hissed.

'Well, you're wrong on all counts!' she said fuming. 'John's nothing other than my lawyer and my friend—'

'And stays the night with you.'

'Once. Because I was upset,' she yelled. 'And he left at three. He comforted me—'

'All innocent? Never made love to you?' Leon queried in frank disbelief.

'*No!*'

'Never *touched* you?'

'Umm…'

Her eyes flickered. And she found herself being lifted, Leon's fury carrying her halfway across the room before she could gather any kind of protest together.

'He kisses you. He touches you. So can I!' he hissed, pausing in mid-stride.

Then his head descended and the fires ignited more fiercely than ever. She did her best to grit her teeth and stop herself from coiling her hands around his neck in compliance. And somehow she summoned up the strength—and the voice—to protest.

'Don't treat me like this! You have no right!'

His eyes silvered. His reply was a burning kiss which softened and sweetened, becoming so tender that she thought her heart would break with sorrow. Still holding that kiss, transfixing her with dreams of what might have been, he began to move towards the bedroom again.

He felt drunk. Unable to believe he was acting so badly. But he couldn't stomach the thought of Sefton…

He felt her gasp and gentled the pressure of his mouth which had become fierce and bruising again. Gently he swept his lips over her jaw, hating his weakness for her, unable to understand why she aroused such explosive emotions in him when he'd always been rational and considerate to a fault.

But emotions there were. Pity. Anger. Compassion, jealousy—oh, God, the jealousy! And such fevered desire… His mouth caressed her high cheekbone, the sight of her half-closed eyes making his pulses race. Reverently he kissed each quivering lid and exulted in her throaty moan.

His shins suddenly hit the bed, jarring his body and he fell with her onto the soft quilt, his senses befogged by the heady perfume of roses somewhere in the room.

'Tell me no,' he said huskily, covering her body with his.

'Nnnnoooo,' she whispered languorously.

'Not totally convincing.'

Lazily he let his fingers trail across the soft warm skin just above the waistband of her skirt. She jerked and writhed and he caught her arms to imprison her, letting his mouth swoop and mimic the caress of his fingers while she gasped in pleasure, her legs wrapping around his body while she pleaded implausibly for him to stop.

So he did. And she blinked several times, her mouth sulky with disappointment. He waited, his breath locked in his lungs, his eyes fierce with desire.

Feebly she tried to hit him, forgetting her legs were keeping his body close to hers, and then she muttered something angrily and wrenched free, tumbling with him on the bed, over and over, kissing and moaning, tangled with him in a hungry desperation as hands and mouths and teeth and limbs strained to ease the explosion of longing.

Beneath him she moved in her old, wanton way, her eyes luring, her body firing him to unbelievable abandon. She was everywhere, her hair teasing his cheek, her yielding body urgently thrashing with his, her mouth wandering at his throat and her heart beating violently against his chest.

He wanted to devour her whole, to take her in and make her his. To wipe away all other men she'd known and to leave just the memory of his body, his mouth, the pleasure he could give her.

Her tongue slicked along his collar-bone and he shuddered.

'I want you so badly,' he croaked.

Her mouth opened and no sound emerged. So he kissed it, the sweet pressure bringing an ache to his heart. He looked at her with dark hunger in his eyes and knew he had smashed her resistance. His mouth enclosed hers, his tongue tasting her as he slid his hand to the top of her thigh and met warm, wet silk.

Emma cried out, a needy cry that brought an answering

spear of need in him. Rhythms pounded mercilessly in every part of his body: the thud of her heart and his, the movement of her hands over his back and the leaping, dangerous pulse of heat beneath his fingers which called to a deep answering pulse within his very manhood.

Her throat arched, his mouth urgently moved there, branding it with searing kisses. And then he lifted her, crazed with her, intoxicated and utterly incapable of anything other than actions of raw instinct. In a fierce movement he'd pulled off her T-shirt and had shrugged away his shirt, pulling her to him.

Skin on skin. Thunder roared in his ears. It was unbelievable. The feel of her. The softness...

She moved in a deliberately provocative way, an insistent gesture which she repeated, the hard peaks of her breasts describing a circle against his chest and its shuddering muscles.

'Kiss,' she moaned, taking one breast between her hands and offering it to him.

Every cell in his body reacted. With a deep, visceral groan, he lowered his mouth and took the dark, pulsing nipple in his mouth. Emma jerked as his tongue flickered and tasted and she grabbed at his hair when he closed his eyes in bliss and suckled greedily.

'Other one.'

Without gentleness, she dragged his head from her breast to satisfy its twin, his nose and chin deep in the lushly cushioned mound.

'Touch me again,' she whispered.

Instead, he brought her hand to ease his own agony. And she understood, always had, knowing what she did to him and that something between them blazed so fiercely that no man, not even Leon, could keep under control.

At her touch, he bucked and drew back, his eyes glazed with passion. Gently he unbuttoned her skirt and eased down the frivolous blue briefs inch by inch over her glorious thighs.

For a brief moment he buried his face in the golden triangle of hair, promising himself greater delights later. She uttered little moans of pleasure as his mouth enclosed her sweetness and then she was kicking off her briefs with frantic legs.

And then, when he fumbled with his own belt, she reached up. She seemed to be in a mist, as if a veil had drifted over his eyes, and her body simmered before him, beautiful and golden in its nakedness but annoyingly out of focus.

Then he felt her remove the rest of his clothes, gasping his name when he was kneeling above her, naked too. Gently she took him between her hands, but he couldn't bear the waiting.

'No. I want *you*,' he urged breathily.

'Leon…'

'Now!'

'Oh, yes,' she cried and pulled him down, arching up to him, demanding his mouth, her arms guiding, helping him to slip into that paradise…

'Emma!'

He didn't know if he'd spoken aloud or not. Didn't care. Silky liquid enclosed him, warm, tight, exquisite, each gentle movement a sweet torment. But Emma didn't want gentleness. Her hands grasped his muscled buttocks and urged him on.

His body took over. In the back of his mind he knew he'd meant to pleasure her slowly, to drive her wild with desire. But this was too much. His mouth lunged at hers and his rhythm increased, primitive, long and deep thrusts which seemed to strip his mind of everything but the sensation that they were joined as one person and would never be parted.

Tears wet his face. Emma. Emma, Emma, called his aching heart and she was calling him, crying his name over and over again, gasping into his mouth, licking his salty tears—or were they hers?—and all the time the volcanic emotions in his body were rising, higher, higher, the heat and sweat and total sense of freedom and release making him yell with her as they rolled around the bed. And his movements became shorter, harder, faster. Their voices deeper, huskier. Kisses fiercer. Hands more frantic.

It was happening. Shooting up through his body like a torrent, flames of heat burning his skin, each pore electrified, faster, faster...

'Emma, *Emma*!' he yelled.

But she was silent, shuddering, jerking, a seraphic smile on her face. He realised he'd come down to earth again though they were still united and he wanted to keep it that way, warm, tingling, the sweetest feeling in the world. The sweetest woman.

He smiled back. She sighed deeply and her eyes closed, her entire body limp. Carefully he eased himself over her so that he bore most of his own weight, and snuggled up, his face close to hers. Still linked, he thought muzzily. If only that could be true for ever.

His brain wasn't working too well. It was a moment before a slow frown found the energy to work a line between his brows. What had he wished? Confused, he gave himself up to gazing at her. It was sex talking. Nothing else.

He eased away.

'Don't go,' she mumbled incoherently, her arm flapping in vague protest.

But he felt ice clutch at his heart. And swung around so he was sitting on the edge of the chaotic bed, his hand clearing his eyes of...someone's tears. Hence his blurred vision. And he was gritting his teeth. Finding his brain. It was in there somewhere. His pulses still galloped mercilessly but they'd soon calm down.

Eyeing the distance involved, he made a good stab at lurching towards the bathroom.

'Wharr-you-doin'?' Emma slurred.

'Shower.'

Her mutter showed she didn't think much of that but he

grimly staggered to it and turned it to cold. Taking a deep breath, he stepped in, suffering his penance.

Better if he'd done this before, not after. How could he have been such a prat? The freezing needles of water seemed to wake him up out of his stupor. So what kind of man makes love to a woman he despises?

Marina was right. This was the woman who'd single-handedly destroyed his family business without regard for the consequences, sparing no thought for the hundreds of people she'd left without the security they'd planned for.

Recompensing those people had broken his father and had hastened his death and, Leon reflected grimly, it had given *him* sixteen-hour days and no social life while he'd built up the family fortunes again, scheming, planning, networking, and begging for investment. He slapped his fist into his palm. This was also the woman who drove his brother to a terrible and violent death.

And he'd just made love to her.

'You'll get pneumonia!'

He looked up. Through the curtain of water he could see her, a sheet wrapped around her incomparable body. Her fingers were testing the temperature of the water and she was looking at him in sheer amazement.

He discovered that he was shivering violently and stepped out, his eyes blazing so black and hard that she took a step back.

Grabbing a towel, he snarled, 'I don't care.'

She cringed against the tiled wall. 'Leon..!' she whispered in shock.

From under ferocious brows he scowled. 'It's done. A mistake. Can't be undone,' he said shortly, grabbing towels to warm him.

And he wanted to wound her as he was wounded, ripped apart by desire for her, his self-respect torn to shreds and left bleeding on that rumpled bed. His head came up. Rivulets of water poured down his face from his saturated hair and he mopped at them with the end of the towel. He wanted her to see his eyes and the loathing there.

'It got a bit out of hand, didn't it?' he said, mimicking her pitiful excuse earlier.

She gasped. 'Get dressed and get out,' she whispered.

'My *pleasure*,' he growled, towelling vigorously.

She left. He heard her collapse on the bed. Wondered if she was all right. And checked himself. She was a big girl. She could look after herself, only too well.

Then he remembered he had to get his clothes from the bedroom. As he gathered them up, finding they'd been hurled into odd places with surprising force and distance, he glanced at her surreptitiously.

She lay curled up in a ball just like Lexi and for a moment his heart lurched before he could steady it again. She was very still, her face almost hidden in her shielding arms.

'My shirt's underneath you,' he said coldly.

She didn't move and he was forced to lift her hips. He looked at her sharply. Tremors were rippling through her entire body.

'Emma?'

'Go away!'

He hesitated. 'Do you need medicine or something?'

She sat up with a sudden violence, her eyes spitting fire. 'Yes. I need love. I need a man who doesn't use me. Do you know what you've done, Leon? Do you?'

'Yes,' he said bleakly. 'Do you? Or do you think you had no part in what happened, no input, no desire?'

'Don't,' she muttered, covering her face with her hands.

He pulled them away. 'Look at me.'

When she did, he wished he hadn't asked. Her eyes reproached him, making him feel ashamed of himself. He made a helpless gesture with his hands. He didn't understand what was happening to him, only that they couldn't be near one another.

'The truth is, Emma,' he said tightly, 'we're destroying

each other. This can't go on. We have to separate or...' He paused, fighting for breath.

'Or what?' she whispered.

'Get each other out of our systems. There'll never be a middle way for us, Emma. You know that, I know that. So it's in my bed, or out of the country—and the choice is yours.'

'I—I'm not ready to leave! Lexi doesn't know—'

'You've seen your child. You know she'll be fine with me. I'll find some way of solving Lexi's need for parents.'

'What?' she cried.

'I don't know. But...' He couldn't believe he was saying this, that he was urging her to leave. He wanted her so much that every bone in his body was aching. 'Do the decent thing and get on the next plane,' he said in a strangled tone. And the jealousy surfaced, searing and bitter in his gut. 'Ring Sefton and take him with you. He's desperate to give you what you want. If he hasn't done so already.'

'What is it with you about John?' she cried hotly. 'Are you jealous or something?'

'Yes,' he yelled, grabbing her shoulders. 'I don't want anyone else to touch you but me. It sickens me to think of other men making love to you. And it crucifies me to want you. It degrades me—'

'And if I was innocent?' she said bitterly.

'But you're not.'

'If.'

His mouth tightened but he couldn't prevent the wishing from showing in his eyes. 'It's not worth discussing,' he said gratingly. 'I want you out of here in the morning. Make your arrangements.'

It was hard, leaving. His feet were unwilling—his whole body, too. But he got out eventually, her words still ringing in his head. *'If I was innocent.'* He sucked in a shuddering breath, every muscle in his body screaming as he tried to get that idea out of his mind. Because the implications were too alarming to contemplate.

CHAPTER TEN

EMMA rested. She would need all her strength if she was to fight for what she wanted: to clear her name and to be accepted as Lexi's mother. And then...she shut her mind to that. But Leon's jealousy had given her hope.

Later, she rang John and he came over. They went out to a taverna in the nearby beach resort of Alikes and she thought how much Lexi would enjoy being here, with a different pony and trap clip-clopping and rumbling past every few minutes.

John seemed pleased that she was leaving the villa and arranged to pick up her things in the morning. He wasn't so pleased when she said she was going to lay siege to Leon's house till he let her see her daughter.

'Abduct her and let's get home,' he advised.

Emma stared at him in shock. 'I couldn't possibly,' she protested, putting down a forkful of red mullet. 'She doesn't know me. She'd be terrified—'

'Oh, she'll soon get used to you,' he said airily.

'No, John. I'm not doing that to my daughter. How can you suggest that?'

He took her hand and looked into her eyes. 'To save you distress,' he said gently. 'Poor Emma. This must be awful for you. You must be at your wits' end—'

'Don't make me a victim, John,' she said with a frown, suddenly sensing that he'd always done that. 'I'm determined to see this through properly.'

'But why?' he argued. 'When we can be up and off in

148

twenty-four hours? You with your kid, just as you wanted it? She'll be OK. Kids can get used to anything—'

'No.'

She removed her hand, suddenly disliking his sweaty touch. How could he be so insensitive to Lexi's needs?

'So you're going to camp outside Kyriakis's place, hoping to catch a glimpse of her as they drive out—and you think that's going to bring you and her closer together?' he said sarcastically.

'It won't come to that,' she said firmly. 'Leon won't be able to cope with the scandal of his sister-in-law parked on his doorstep like a lost parcel.'

'I thought I was here to give you advice?' John said sulkily.

'You are.' She patted his arm consolingly, feeling bad that she'd dragged him over and had taken no notice of him since. He had devoted an extraordinary amount of time to her. 'I'm terribly grateful for what you've done. But John, I did make it clear that I'd never take Lexi until she was happy in my company.'

He caught her hand and kissed it, holding it fast when she tried to retrieve it. 'Emma, I wish you'd listen to me. Let's do it. If you won't take your daughter now, then you must see she'll never be yours. From what you tell me, Kyriakis has established himself in Lexi's heart. Isn't that true?'

'Ye-e-es,' she said slowly.

'He's going to make this as difficult as possible. And my enquiries here suggest that you won't make much headway legally. You'd be condemned to flying over here once, perhaps twice, a year and being faced with a child who doesn't want to be with you. I know this is painful, but I think you should give up. Come back to England and start a new life. Emma,' he declared, his eyes shining, 'let me take care of you. I can heal your pain. I'd do anything for you.'

Her eyes widened. Leon had been right! Appalled that she'd given out the wrong messages to John, she searched for a gentle let-down. And in searching she let her gaze swing absently to the taverna opposite.

Where Leon sat, glaring. She gulped. Of course. She was constantly being watched—in case she did something to ruin the wretched Kyriakis name. Like steal a child's ice cream or something, she thought waspishly.

John's eyes narrowed. Following her glance, he saw Leon and let her hand drop. 'Now, that's an opportunity I can't miss. I'll go and have a word,' he said casually.

Emma blinked. He'd always been edgy about meeting Leon before. 'About what?'

'Oh, tell him you're leaving the villa, where you'll be, that kind of thing.'

He seemed to take a long time about it. She'd worked her way through a rolled filo pastry pudding and a chocolate ice cream before he came back. Leon had listened to John without moving a muscle, his dark eyes menacing.

'That's done,' her lawyer said with satisfaction. 'Ready to go back?'

She would have liked a walk along the beach perhaps, but presumed he must have things to do. 'Sure. I'll have an early night.'

'Me too.'

It wasn't until she was fighting off John's attentions on the doorstep of the villa that she realised he'd expected her early night to include him.

'No, John,' she cried in panic, grappling with him. 'Don't spoil everything—'

'Come on. We're great together. When you were in my arms the other night—'

'You were comforting me,' she protested, leaning back till she felt her spine would crack. This was like Taki all over again. She felt herself weaken as terror struck through her, fuelled by the terrible memories of her husband's abuse. '*Please*, John,' she whimpered desperately.

'Leave her alone, Sefton,' came Leon's quiet and ominously calm voice.

Emma breathed a sigh of utter relief as John's vice-like grip eased. She would be all right. Surveillance had its advantages after all.

'Keep out of this,' snarled John, his face distorted with rage.

Leon came right up to them. 'Let her go, or you'll find yourself on the next plane to England. With your own personal resuscitation team,' he said pleasantly.

Emma was immediately released. She moved away, rubbing her arms.

'Goodnight, Sefton,' murmured Leon. Muttering, John stalked to his car and Leon turned his hooded eyes on her. 'All right?' She nodded dumbly. He held out his hand. 'Key.'

Trembling, she fumbled uselessly in her bag. And dropped it, and its contents onto the path. They both bent to gather everything up. Leon, inches away, looked into her eyes.

'Are you really all right, Emma?' he asked huskily.

'Shaken up. Disappointed,' she admitted. 'I know. You told me so.' She stood up. 'But thank you. It saved an ugly scene.' She shuddered.

Leon put an arm around her shoulder. 'And Sefton's manhood is intact,' he observed with a wry smile, unlocking the door and switching on the lights for her.

She allowed herself a faint smile too. 'I would definitely have kneed him,' she agreed jerkily.

'Can you manage or do you want me to stay?' he asked neutrally.

'I'll be fine once I've got my breath back. It—it happened to me once before, that's why I panicked. I wasn't so lucky that time.'

Leon's jaw clenched. He hesitated for so long that her heart began to beat erratically, and then he turned away and began to walk down the path, giving a brief wave of his hand as he did so.

* * *

Awake early, she tidied and cleaned the villa and left her stuff in an empty shed which she'd seen when they'd been feeding the animals. She stuck a note on the door to her lawyer that was brief and to the point. 'Will be in touch. Have found accommodation. Emma.'

She hadn't, of course, but she'd do that later, once she'd wrung concessions from Leon.

It wasn't till she'd almost reached his house that she remembered he was having a heart-to-heart with Marina that morning, and wouldn't thank her if she turned up in the middle of it.

So she sat down in the orchard amongst the wild fennel and oats and daisies, and idly watched clouded yellow butterflies flitting about. After a while she felt a little restless and set off for a walk.

Ahead, half veiled in a mist, sprawled the mountains, grey-green from the thousands of olives which clad their sides. Small hills rose from the flat valley floor in front, their tops crowned with pencil cypress and low white buildings.

This was all of Leon's land. Each plant irrigated, tended lovingly, the cherry, fig, apricot and almond trees making little islands in the sea of currant vines and small hay fields. She came across a field of melons and, beside it, a field of scarlet poppies. Lizards basked on a stone well-head and chickens—chittens, she thought with a lump in her throat—ran about the undergrowth.

She leaned against the trunk of an olive tree whose girth suggested it must be several centuries old and felt a love for the island steal over her, catching her unawares. She tried not to love it, tried to find flaws. Wrong language. Strange letters unlike any alphabet she'd ever known and hadn't yet mastered. Miles from home, the culture she knew.

That was all she could come up with. Not a lot. Could she live here? Her heart and her head told her that Lexi would be happier on the island. And she… She inhaled slowly and let the breath out again. She wanted to be Lexi's mother properly, not just for weekends.

There was something more. She wanted Leon too. But she'd already realised that, since he held her responsible for destroying his family, their relationship could only be based on sexual attraction. Though that was a start. And it was the only thing she had going for her.

Her pulses raced at the very thought. He hadn't been shocked by her damaged breast—hadn't even mentioned it. He must want her very much to have ignored the scar.

Maybe, as her lover, he'd listen to her when she tried to explain about Taki and her role as financial director. Her brow furrowed. Problem was, there wasn't any evidence for that. It would be her word against that of a Kyriakis. Not much hope there, she thought gloomily. Her eyes glinted. But she had to try.

When she checked her watch and found it was lunch-time she decided to head back. She'd walked a long way and by the time she arrived at the front of Leon's house—it had to be the front, for maximum embarrassment to him—she was not only very tired but the sky had clouded over and drops of rain were beginning to fall.

She took a deep breath and knocked on the door. It was opened not by Natasa but by Leon.

'Yes?'

'I've come to see Lexi,' she said humbly.

'Not today, thank you.'

'OK.' She sat down as the door was closing and prepared for a long wait. But the door opened almost immediately.

'What are you doing?'

'Waiting,' she said over her shoulder.

'For?'

'You to change your mind.'

'It's raining.'

'I've noticed,' she said gravely.

The door closed. Emma muttered something to the Fates

who'd chosen to make today of all days the time they let the heavens open, and she put her bag on her head in a vain attempt to keep the rain off. It didn't help. The water ran over it and onto her knees.

Thunder cracked, making her jump. And almost immediately there was a lightning flash. The Fates then decided to make a good job of washing the island and instead of rain they produced a wall of water which hit her with such force that she was reduced to crouching in a miserable heap while the torrent beat the ground ferociously and thus flung red soil up at her.

She was soaked through in minutes. And then suddenly the rain ceased. She looked up cautiously and saw a giant coloured umbrella above her.

'Get inside,' yelled Leon above the pyrotechnics of the storm which was still raging beyond the umbrella.

Oh, hurray, she thought gleefully. And scuttled in.

'You look appalling.'

'Thanks,' she said ruefully, her face glistening with water.

He glared. 'Every time I decide something, you sabotage it.'

'I'm very sorry,' she said, doing her humble bit again.

'Upstairs with you,' he growled. 'Have a bath and get warm.'

'Thank-you-very-much,' she murmured.

'Not funny.'

It was, she thought. Her first goal had been achieved. Shivering, she meekly followed him up the stairs though she was so weary that he reached the top long before she did and he waited impatiently, his fingers drumming on the banister.

'Look at you,' he scolded.

She did. Drenched, her body shedding cinnamon-coloured mud and water, her hair plastered to her head, she knew she must look a sight. The carpet must be in a similar condition too. Guiltily she turned to check and saw the wet red earth trail leading back to the front door.

'Oh, crikey.'

'Wait there.'

He clamped his lips together and turned on his heel while she slumped and dripped. Returning, he held out an enormous bath sheet and wrapped it around her like a cocoon. And then he picked her up, carrying her mummified body through a vast and breathtakingly beautiful bedroom and into a bathroom beyond where he deposited her on the sea-blue tiles.

'I'll find some clothes for you. They'll be in the bedroom. Come down when you're done.'

She nodded, not daring to say anything in case it offended him. She felt shattered but peculiarly perky and her mouth was liable to run away with her for sheer elation. Wriggling out of the bath sheet she locked the door, ran the bath and peeled off her wet things.

After selecting some expensive-looking herbal bath oil, she emptied a prodigious amount of it into the deepening water, turned off the taps and slid in with a sigh. Her head nestled back against a padded headrest. The bath was wide enough for two people side by side, she thought muzzily.

Her eyes closed as her brain considered that fact. Perhaps this was the moment when she'd fall asleep and Leon would break the door down and come crashing in, afraid she'd drowned.

She stayed soaking for ages, half hoping he might do just that but eventually common sense told her that he hadn't had that grumpy face for nothing and he wouldn't break that lovely panelled door anyway.

So she got out, dried herself slowly, wishing someone else could do that for her, and padded into the bedroom to see what delectable item he'd pinched from Marina's wardrobe. It was a man's shirt and jeans.

Ignoring them, she prowled around looking for a hairdryer but didn't find one and had to content herself with wrapping a small towel around her wet hair like a turban.

There was a rap on the door. It was sharp and imperious and she knew it must be him.

'Are you dressed?'

She hoicked the bath sheet around her more securely. 'Near enough,' she replied, and sat down heavily on the bed, her limbs far too tired to help her to stand.

He came in and sat in an easy chair. 'I thought you ought to know. Marina's left with Soula and Natasa. She spoke to her father and he was happy to have his daughters and granddaughter back in the family home.'

'And his wife?'

'She says she can cope if Natasa is there, exercising her calming influence. Anton Christofides is turning a wing of his house into a large, self-contained apartment so they won't move in immediately.'

Emma blinked, not knowing what she should say. 'Was there a scene?'

'Not when I told her I'd settle a large sum on her,' he said cynically.

'Generous.'

'She's irritating and difficult but I feel great sympathy for her,' he muttered. 'She had a child when she was just a frightened kid herself, and a husband who didn't love her.'

'Where's she gone in the meantime?' Emma asked, touched by his compassion.

'To the villa—temporarily. It was her design. I told her she ought to take that up professionally. She's talented. Natasa thinks so too. Marina was quite excited at the prospect.'

'Good,' Emma said warmly.

'Where are *you* staying?' he barked.

Emma shifted, longing to curl up properly on the bed but she was worried that he might think she was issuing an invitation.

'Nowhere. Yet.'

He looked out of the window where the storm was still

raging. 'You can't go out in this.' She remained mute. There wasn't much she could say and the warmth of the bath was making her sleepy. 'What are your intentions, Emma?' he snapped.

'Go to sleep,' she mumbled and let herself fall back to the pillow.

Somewhere in the dim recesses of her mind she heard him muttering under his breath and the cool whisper of linen being draped over her tired body. And then she fell into a dark and deep well of sleep.

It seemed a few moments later when she woke. The rain was still falling in torrents outside and it seemed to be night. She yawned and stretched, then froze. A pair of eyes were looking at her.

A light snapped on and the eyes turned into Leon. 'Hungry?' he muttered, looking wonderfully tousled and grumpy.

She wondered if he'd been there all the time and gave a little shiver. 'Umm…yes, I am, Leon.'

'I found a hairdryer for you. Come down when you've used it,' he said curtly. 'And stop being Miss Meek and Mild. I prefer you to shout and laugh.'

She grinned and sat up, prepared to do either of those if necessary, but he'd gone.

It took ages to sort her hair because it had dried in coiled lumps inside the towel. But eventually it looked good enough. She couldn't say that for the rest of her.

Leon's shirt needed the sleeves turned up till there was a huge roll of material at her elbows. If she fastened the top button then the collar dug into her neck every time she looked down and if she left it open the shirt gaped a bit. She opted for gaping.

Beneath the knee-length shirt, the jeans collected in sad folds above her bare feet and it had taken all her efforts to make the belt hold up the weight of all that unsupported denim.

'Hallo? Here I am,' she called, standing uncertainly in the empty hall.

Leon appeared after a moment, looked her up and down, did his famous scowl and turned back, indicating she should follow him with a curt flip of his hand.

'Feta cheese salad,' he said abruptly, when they'd fetched up in a large kitchen.

'Lovely.'

She beamed, and tucked in, looking around. Expensive floor tiles, coffered ceiling and royal-blue wooden cupboards. A marble table, comfortable chairs and three wrought-iron candelabra. Murano glass downlighter adorned with angels. Stylish objects—a piece of driftwood, a large shell, a wooden bowl of realistic artificial cherries—casually placed as if by accident, but looking absolutely right. Gorgeous. If this was another sample of Marina's taste, then she'd make a great interior designer.

Leon cleared his throat and she looked up expectantly.

'You'll have to stay here tonight and don't say, Yes, Leon.'

She stopped herself from giggling at his monotone delivery. She was in for the night. Goal number two!

'Thank you,' she murmured and decided to go for gold. 'Have you worked out how to help Lexi with her parent problem?' she asked innocently.

He scowled beautifully. 'No.'

She tried not to look pleased and set about rubbing salt in his wounds. 'Poor kiddie. She's such a sweetie and it'll be awful seeing her become more and more paranoid—'

'Emma,' he roared, banging his fist on the table and making her—and the crockery—jump. 'I'm worried stiff. You're not helping—'

'I am, I can,' she said earnestly. 'You know why I'm here, don't you?'

'Because you're an obstinate, difficult, stroppy, mule of a

woman who doesn't know when the odds are stacked against you,' he growled.

'Well, yes, there's that,' she conceded smugly.

He glared. 'And?'

Now the moment had come, she was losing courage. It was such an outrageous suggestion in the cold light of a kitchen.

'This is…so difficult,' she said, twiddling her fork in the salad aimlessly.

'That's never stopped you before,' Leon said caustically.

Her mouth twitched. No. It hadn't. She leapt where angels feared to tread.

'OK,' she said, but keeping her eyes lowered on her frantic fork. 'I have a proposition.' There was a silence and in that silence she suddenly noticed her desperately unsexy clothes. They wouldn't help at all. Putting her fork down, she clasped her hands in front of her and managed to undo another button. 'Well,' she began, letting her hands fall to her lap.

'Yes?'

It was only a small, barely spoken word, but it had carried heat and lust and passion. And when her eyes flickered up, she rocked back, knocked breathless by the sizzling impact of his sensual expression.

He would agree, she thought, tense with excitement. Her hands shook.

'You offered me a choice,' she said huskily.

Something quivered in the muscles of his face, as if each one had tightened in sequence. She had to lick her lips or she wouldn't have been able to continue. And it was so important. Her tongue slicked over them again, and the simmering darkness of his eyes dried her throat. Pools of heat were making her focus on her hungering body and she had to redouble her efforts to speak.

'I—' She swallowed, wanting to hurl herself across the table and ravish him, to tear off his shirt and ease the tempestuous turmoil claiming her entire system. 'I said once I'd do anything for Lexi. I imagine you would, too.' He nodded slowly. 'She needs to know me, we've already agreed that. And I understand why you want me to leave…' Agitated because he sat there without saying anything, other than the hot message he was projecting from every inch of his body, she staggered to her feet and began to pace up and down the kitchen. Her physical urges had to go somewhere. Her brows drew together. 'I've forgotten where I was.'

He seemed to have trouble finding his place in her outburst too. 'You understand why I want you to leave,' he provided eventually.

'Oh, yes. Right. However,' she said, prowling furiously, 'I've decided *not* to leave the island.'

'Ah-h-h.'

It was a whisper. Husky, deep and laced with such feeling that she found her steps getting even faster and infinitely more erratic.

She sucked in a huge breath and launched her suggestion, rattling it off at high speed without giving him a chance to interrupt.

'And, to start with, I want to stay in this house because that'll suit us both. When you think about it, you'll see it makes sense. I will get to know Lexi quicker that way because I can pop up and take a rest whenever I need and yet I'll be around a lot of the time gradually becoming part of Lexi's life, so you'd have to put up with me for a shorter time than if I was commuting. And after a while she'll accept me as her mother and—and she'll be happy and then…then I can leave and find somewhere to live on the island and Lexi will know she has a mother and I can see her often and write to her and telephone…' She ran out of breath and dreams and stopped abruptly.

'You…want to…live in this house?' The silence was deafening, the pause unbearable. 'You know what that means,' he growled. It was her turn to nod, her eyes enormous in her pale face. 'Let me get this straight,' he said, his voice oddly strangled. 'You're saying that, for Lexi's sake, you'd risk being used for sex?'

It wasn't like that, she told herself. It wasn't just sex. Maybe that was *his* attitude towards her at the moment, but she'd convince him of her innocence somehow and then his feelings would change.

It was a huge gamble. But worth going for. She stared at the floor, willing her nerve to hold.

And realised in dismay how stupid she looked. With all the striding about, the jeans had unfolded and hung around her ankles, the belt having given up entirely and having allowed the waistband to slide precariously to her hips so that the crotch appeared somewhere around her calves.

It dawned on her that it hadn't been sexual tension that had put a strain on his muscles. He'd been trying hard not to laugh.

'You...said you'd do anything to get Lexi,' he said in a rasping.

'I did,' she squeaked.

'Even making yourself available in exchange for access?'

She knew that Leon must be trying to discover how far she'd go to be with her daughter. It was the, Will you sleep with me or any other man I might name and, if you will, then you're a slut? kind of question.

She might as well answer. Her hopes of finding the love they'd once shared could now take a running jump. She'd become a figure of ridicule.

'If that's the price,' she mumbled crossly, glaring at the clumsy jeans and hauling them up.

She knew he was looking at her, his stare rooting her to the spot even though her gaze was fixed with unlikely intensity on the floor. The atmosphere burned around Emma as, presumably, Leon battled to stop himself from laughing out loud.

'Agreed,' he said, when she had abandoned all hope of an answer.

'Thank you,' she said in a small voice.

'There's a condition.' He waited but she was too miserable to comment. 'You cut all contact with Sefton. No calls, no visits, no letters, no e-mails—nothing.'

Dubiously she chewed her lip. 'He knows where he stands now, Leon. I still need him as my lawyer here.'

'Lawyer or fellow abductor?' he asked flatly. 'I have details now of the route you've planned. He told me in Alikes yesterday evening. If I were you, I'd forget Sefton and his little games. They could result in you never seeing your daughter again.'

Her eyes rounded in dismay. 'Why would he tell you?' she asked, pink-faced with horrified embarrassment.

'He's been warning me of the possibility ever since my first meeting with him, Emma. He doesn't want you to succeed.'

'Why?' she cried, baffled.

'He doesn't want you saddled with someone else's child, don't you see? And Sefton's the type who needs women to be dependent on them. You filled that bill very well all the time you were in prison and desperate. He played the hero. I'm not denigrating what he did for you, only his motives. The moment you looked like showing strength, he backtracked and did everything he could to make sure you ended up miserable and needy. You're not totally convinced, I can see. But will you believe me if I say that I even know he's brought over clothes and toys for Lexi, to keep her amused during the journey?'

Betrayed, she thought. Her plan would never have worked—John would have seen to that, and Leon would have had her stopped before they even set sail from the island.

She was horrified. 'We made plans...'

'I know.' His eyes were grave.

'I would have lost her for ever.'

'Without doubt.'

'How could he do this to me?'

'He had his own agenda. You were supposed to fit into it.'

She trembled. Choking with dismay, she took a step towards him and tripped over the jeans, grabbing the table in frustrated fury at her own clumsiness.

'You think I meant to whisk her away from everything she loved,' she cried, desperate that he should understand. 'But I wouldn't do anything so cruel. John and I argued about that but I insisted that Lexi and I had a stable and loving relationship before we—we—'

'Snatched her. How could you even think of doing that, Emma?' he asked quietly.

She gulped. 'I told you before,' she wailed. 'John had reported that she was a millstone around your neck. I couldn't bear that, Leon. I thought of my baby, being suffered by you because it was your duty, your wife and daughter treating her badly, and—and it made me *mad*.'

Her vigorous movements had dislodged the jeans again and she muttered curses under her breath as she tried to leash the belt tighter around her middle.

'And now you know different?' he asked throatily.

She flicked a glance at him, ready to complain—if he was laughing—that it wasn't her fault he couldn't find her any female clothes. But his expression was implacable and only his eyes gleamed as if in amusement.

'Now I know different,' she agreed, tossing back her hair and hanging onto the gaping shirt for grim death, 'I have no intention of ever taking her away. She's settled here happily and she loves you. I hope she'll come to love me too. As I said, if all goes well, I'll live on Zakynthos and find a job. I've only ever wanted the best for Lexi. Honest,' she said earnestly. 'I thought I was best. Now I think she needs us both. You can trust me. I swear I won't abduct her.'

He was frowning and she held her breath, then she realised she was dragging the shirt hard over her breasts and he was probably worried that she'd rip the seams or something. Her fingers eased up and so did his frown.

'Believe me,' she pleaded when he just sat there.

He blinked as if he'd been thinking of something entirely different. 'I believe you,' he said slowly. 'But I will take precautions nevertheless. I don't want you to go anywhere without me. I need to watch over you, Emma. This house will be your prison. That's reasonable under the circumstances, isn't it?'

'I've known worse prisons,' she muttered, wriggling uncomfortably in the jeans. 'This one's got a swimming pool.'

His mouth tightened, definitely, she realised, to hide a smile. She sighed. Her appearance was wearing down his resistance. He'd roll about on the floor in hysterics soon.

'Then, you agree.'

'Of course.'

Absently she pushed up the sleeves of the baggy shirt which had flopped down over her hands and had been dangling unappealingly. What did she look like? He'd never want her after this. Bang went goal number three.

'Emma...where are your clothes?' he asked tautly. 'The villa was empty when I dropped Marina there.'

She hitched up the jeans again, longing for a sexy dress with a slit skirt. Or even a dull Auntie Maud dress that fitted her vaguely. Then Leon could stop busting a gut trying not to fall about laughing.

'In a shed near the goats and sheep and things,' she replied meekly.

He grunted. 'They'll have to wait till tomorrow then. I'm not going out in this weather. Are you finishing that?' he asked belligerently, pointing to her mangled salad.

'Not hungry any more,' she replied, subdued.

He scowled. 'Then I'll take you up. You can have Taki's old room. It's not been used and all his stuff's there but I'm sure that won't bother you.'

She glared back at him from under her brows. Was that a

dig, to remind her of what she was supposed to have done? Taki's possessions had been taken from the house the day after she'd asked for a divorce and had been shipped to Zakynthos. Taki had obviously intended to skip the country.

'Why should it?' she said with a shrug. The shirt slipped off her shoulders and she sulkily tugged it back again.

Leon's intake of breath alarmed her in its ferocity. 'Don't do that,' he roared, leaping to his feet.

Her eyes widened in bewilderment. 'Do what?'

'Look sexy in whatever you wear,' he yelled savagely.

Emma's eyes widened even more. 'What, these old things?' she cried, wondering if he was being sarcastic. One glance at his mouth and she knew he wasn't. 'Leon,' she croaked, putting up a defensive hand.

'Oh, no,' he said menacingly, 'you don't get out of your agreement like that.'

And suddenly her back was against the wall, Leon was kissing her, the shirt was slipping and she didn't care and firecrackers were going off in her head.

'Bonfire night,' she mumbled crazily.

'I'm consumed,' he said, breathing hotly in her ear.

She shivered. 'Me too. Take me to bed, Leon.' Looking dazed, he drew back, and then grabbed her hand to pull her to the door. But she resisted. 'Wait a minute.' She wasn't spending a moment longer in the jeans. Couldn't have walked in them anyway. With trembling fingers she unleashed the belt and let them drop to the floor, stepping out suddenly untrammelled.

They began to run. Into the hall, up the stairs, into the bedroom where she had first bathed, slept and changed. There he tore off his clothes and hers, driving her against the door and then, in a tumble of arms and legs, to the thickly carpeted floor.

I love you, she said in her head. And she knew then that she wouldn't settle for an occasional relationship with Lexi, and some lusty sex with Leon whenever she visited. She wanted to live with them both for ever and no one was going to stop her.

Her heart swelled as she kissed him, adoring the feel of his toned skin beneath her mouth. Licking him, tasting, eating... Her hands touched his leaping heat and she gazed lovingly into his eyes.

I love you, they said. His teeth drove into his lower lip as if she'd injured him. Shaking, he caressed her breasts. And then his hands paused. She could feel his palm curving around the deep dent where her scar was and she realised that she'd forgotten about it—and that he couldn't have noticed it at all the last time they'd made love.

He was still, looking at her with shocked eyes. Oh, God! she thought. He finds me ugly. It would be the end. He'd never want her. Never fall in love with her. He'd avoid her like the plague and they'd be strangers, meeting on the doorstep every time she came for Lexi.

She felt tears swim into her eyes. One day she'd be faced with Leon's mistress or his wife...a stepmother for Lex. She couldn't bear it.

She pushed his hands away. 'I disgust you, don't I?' she mumbled unhappily. 'I know it's hideous. But it's still me in here,' she said in a blaze, choking on her tears. 'And if you don't like the way I am then all our problems are solved. You won't be tempted to make love to a woman you despise and I won't be tempted to encourage you.'

CHAPTER ELEVEN

UPSET, she tried to scramble to her feet. He pulled her down again and they struggled for a moment till the tears were overwhelming her and she just lay in a miserable heap, weeping. And she was horribly aware that he was tense and tellingly silent beside her, just staring, not touching, not even comforting her.

'You don't have to say anything,' she mumbled. He was appalled. She could see the horror in his eyes. Blind with tears, she sat up, her hands crossing over her breasts. And she realised that she'd instinctively covered her breasts when they'd made love in the villa. Hence his disgust now. 'Where's Taki's room?' she asked croakily. 'P-point me in the right direction and I'll g-get out of your hair,' she said jerkily through her sobs.

'What...?' He sat up too and cleared his throat. 'What happened?'

'Cancer,' she muttered sulkily.

His intake of breath rasped harshly. 'Emma,' he whispered. 'Was that your illness? Why you get so tired?'

'Yes. Taki's room. Where is it?' she snapped.

Leon was in shock. He'd loved her breasts. They'd been perfect. Softly rounded globes, sweet to his lips, with wonderfully responsive nipples that leapt eagerly into his mouth.

And she'd faced the most terrible disease... He felt a gutwrenching fear empty his gut and cause his stomach to contract fiercely. What was her future? She might *die*! The shock rocketed through him bewilderingly, thundering through his body and leaving it weak. Aghast, he met her wet-lashed eyes and fought his desperate urge to say mad things.

167

Like, *Don't ever leave me, you can't die, why you, of all people?*

'I'm so sorry,' he growled inadequately instead.

She looked at him with pitiful eyes as if her world had come to an end, the tears pouring down her unhappy face.

And whether it was unwise or not, he couldn't let her go. Gently he stroked her arm, trying to ignore his own fear, his own needs, and to concentrate on hers. She thought she was ugly. That he didn't find her sexy any more. He smiled ruefully to himself. If only!

'Take your hands away from your breasts,' he said quietly.

'No.' She shook her head violently. 'You've seen me. Isn't that enough? Do you want to humiliate me more?'

'Seeing isn't enough for either of us.'

Ruthlessly he unpeeled her fingers, wet with salty tears, and kissed every inch of each breast. She winced and jerked back when his mouth brushed the scar but he was too strong for her and after a juddering moment of tension she gave in.

'Is that good?' he murmured.

Emma couldn't believe what was happening. It was good. She let out a low moan, revelling in the glorious feel of his firm lips touching where no one—even she—had touched with such gentle worship.

It made her cry to see him loving her there, devoting delicate, sweet kisses to that cruel slash into her femininity.

'Don't cry,' he murmured, raising his head. 'It's all over now. Isn't it? It is, tell me it's over,' he demanded urgently.

Bewildered, trying to stop her sobs, she found herself being crushed in his arms. He was trembling. She couldn't understand why. And then he'd pushed her back a little, his eyes intent on hers.

'Is it over?' he repeated fiercely.

She felt her heart beat faster. Had she got it wrong *again*? 'Why does it matter so much to you?' she asked breathlessly.

Leon stared. 'I—I'm just asking. It affects Lexi, doesn't it?' he said, sounding irritated.

She hoped it was for another reason too. But she didn't dare to totally trust her intuition. It had been wrong so many times before. Her imagination had leapt to conclusions that were way off the mark.

'I'm in the clear,' she assured him and couldn't mistake the way he sagged in relief. He was stroking her breast again as if his caress could heal it. And perhaps he was right. She did feel whole again. Her delighted smile lit up her face. 'I'm expected to live to one hundred and three providing I don't break my neck doing cartwheels.'

Leon felt his heart buck at her joke. All he wanted to do was to hold her close and block out the moment when he'd thought she, so passionate, such a lover of life, might die before her time. His eyes closed in a fervent prayer of thanks.

When he opened them he saw that she was smiling, but wilting. 'Come to bed,' he said in a gravelly voice. 'And tell me about it.'

Tenderly he pulled back the sheet and helped her in, then joined her, drawing her into his arms and holding her as if she were fragile china.

'When did it happen?' he asked quietly. 'You looked pretty rough when I visited you in prison. Was it then?'

'Well, the shock of being charged with fraud can't have helped, and I'd felt too sick with worry to eat, but it had started before then. Though I didn't discover the lump till I *was* in prison. The oncologist talked to me and said it could have been due to the stress of my marriage...'

She clamped her lips together but he put a questing finger beneath her chin and lifted it so that she was forced to meet his eyes.

'What stress?' he asked grimly.

'You won't want to know. Leave it. Best unsaid.'

'No. I don't want there to be any secrets, Emma. The time for that is past.'

She lowered her lashes but his finger was insistent and made her look at him again.

'I have to know,' he said gently, his eyes soft with compassion.

'I made an awful mistake,' she said sadly. 'Taki was very sweet and attentive when I was getting over you. I suppose I fell for him because he seemed to have some of your characteristics. But once we were married I realised that he was obsessively jealous of you, and had married me just to hurt you. I told him that was crazy, you'd dumped me.'

'He was right. It did hurt me,' he said, living that pain again. He'd hated his brother then, and had been ashamed of himself for feeling that way. It had seemed as if Emma had betrayed him, but logic told him that she had a right to fall in love with anyone she fancied. 'You say he was jealous?' It was news to him.

'He talked about you all the time,' she admitted. 'It didn't help our relationship. I kept comparing you two.'

Something leapt within him. 'Oh?' he enquired casually.

'Leon…I think you should know that he didn't like you much. He thought his father favoured you. Teachers, friends…everyone.'

He was stunned. 'I never knew. Go on.'

She bit her lip. 'Oh. Well…our relationship went downhill.'

It seemed she'd come to a halt in her story. 'That was the stress?' he asked with a frown. 'I can see it was tough being married to someone you didn't love, but not that bad, surely?' His eyes narrowed as he read the expression in her eyes. 'There's something else, isn't there?'

'He was…rough.'

Leon's throat dried. 'How rough?' he growled.

'He got drunk. Because he felt such a failure compared with you,' she explained. 'And he'd come home and shout and fling things and sometimes he'd hit me and—'

Again the compression of her lips. God. Taki had struck her! He thought of her body being bruised, the fear on her face, the misery she must have suffered and could hardly contain his anger. 'And?' he prompted ominously.

She jerked her head away, her eyes lowered. 'He—he made me sleep with him when I didn't want to.'

His chest expanded with a huge, indrawn breath that rasped at his lungs like a saw. 'You mean he raped you?' he asked, clenching his fists in fury.

'Only the once,' she said, ridiculously down-playing what had been a sickening moment.

'Oh, Emma!' He groaned.

'No. I'm not a victim, I refuse to be. I'm not making light of what he did, but he's not going to ruin my life because of his jealous, drunken assault,' she said quietly. 'I've blocked it out of my mind. I don't like to think about it. The past had some nightmare moments and I can only move on and keep fit if I put it aside and look to the future.'

'You're amazing,' he found himself saying in wonder.

She sighed and snuggled up, nuzzling her face into his neck. He couldn't believe what she'd gone through. A rush of feeling filled his head, demanding that he protect her from harm in the future. She wouldn't suffer any more. She'd had enough, he vowed.

'How did you feel when you were told you had cancer?' he asked quietly.

'Terrified. It was like walking into a brick wall. I have no recollection of the rest of that day at all. I was terribly emotional and went into a state of total depression, with days of crying.'

'You were scared of dying,' he said sympathetically.

'No. Of not seeing Lexi,' she cried. 'The only thing I feared was that I'd die without ever seeing her again. That's when I decided that come hell or high water I'd see her and form a relationship with her. So I set about making myself well. And here I am and now you know why I'm so determined that she should know I am her mother.'

'She will. I'll make sure of that,' he said, terribly moved

by her fortitude. Lesser women would have crumpled. Not Emma. His mind whirled with admiration. She deserved success. 'One day, very soon, she will call you Mummy.'

'Leon.' She flung her arms around his neck, her eyes alight with joy. 'You really mean that?'

'Only,' he protested, pretending to choke, 'if I'm not throttled first.'

Hastily she withdrew her arms. 'I went too far again, didn't I?'

'You did.' Laughing, he kissed her slowly and sweetly. 'And now, let's see if you can go too far in another direction.'

'Oh, Mr Kyriakis,' she whispered, hugely demure and fluttering her eyelashes frantically. 'I thought you'd never ask.'

He laughed again. 'Wait there.'

'Where are you going?' she protested, as he clambered out of bed and grabbed his dressing gown for decency.

'We're going to celebrate.'

'Celebrate what?' she asked.

He looked at her, golden and glowing, her skin so flawless, hair gleaming, eyes bright, and he could hardly breathe. Swallowing the extraordinary lump of emotion, he said softly, 'Your life.'

She beamed. 'That's lovely, Leon. I'll drink to that.'

He was out of the room before she could say anything else. As he ran down the stairs he felt his spirits soar. Amazing, he mused, hauling a bottle of champagne from the cold store, how the probing finger of death could put life into perspective.

He knew now that he wanted Emma. Wanted her to stay and live with him, to be in his bed.

Eagerly he raced up the stairs again, two flutes and the champagne in his hand.

'I've gone off the boil,' she said haughtily.

'No problem,' he said with a grin.

The bottle would have been nicely shaken up from all that

running. Aiming it warily at the bathroom door, he eased the cork out. It exploded very satisfactorily and, as Emma squealed with excitement, he let it foam all over her, dragging back the covers to do a thorough job.

'Brute. Look at the bed. And it's all over me.' She gasped.

'So it is,' he said in satisfaction, his voice suddenly husky as he leaned over her, and began to lick it off. He shrugged out of his robe and let his body slide over hers, enjoying her look of mute, shocked delight. 'Perhaps,' he said, almost losing his voice entirely as he began to work over her glistening skin, 'you could do the same for me.'

It took a long time. And he never finished. Before he'd even reached her knees she'd captured a crucial part of his anatomy in her hands and was stroking with such maddeningly strong rhythms that he couldn't bear waiting any longer.

He felt a great tenderness as he made love to her. Almost as if his heart was filled to overflowing with something intangible. The physical sensations were just as intense, his passion for her as volcanic, but an undefinable quality had entered their loving. Something profound and bewildering, a feeling of warmth and contentment. A feeling of coming home.

He kissed her deep scar with great gentleness, wanting to take away all the pain it had ever contained. She shuddered with pleasure and the gaze she turned on him all but tore his heart asunder.

'I love you,' she whispered.

Her mouth met his. For a moment he didn't—couldn't—respond. And then, swept away in an emotion he couldn't explain, he kissed her back with a fierce poignancy that powered its way through his body until only physical energy could scatter its bitter-sweet pain.

Their bodies were one. Every breath they took, every beat of their hearts, every sigh. Gently, with agonising slowness, he moved within her, showering her face with kisses as he did so, his hands caressing each swollen breast.

He began to lose his mind, crazy thoughts darting through his brain. That they would be like this for ever. That he would do anything to make her stay, whatever her past. That this was love for him too. He wanted it to be. So badly. And he let himself pretend it was, because the mere thinking of it intensified his feelings and both fired and delighted his shuttered heart.

Lying beside her afterwards, hearing her breathe, made him happier than he could ever remember. He watched as she fell asleep, kissing her nose on impulse and getting a grunt for his pains.

If he loved her, he thought soberly, his conscience was in for a bumpy ride. He had to talk to her, see if there was anything in her claim that she was innocent. Find evidence. But how?

Three weeks was a long time in politics. It was also a long time in a child's life, Emma thought happily as she and Leon walked along the flower-decked street in pretty Alikes, with Lexi grasping their hands and being given swings in the air.

'One, two, three…wheee!' she and Leon went.

'Again,' demanded Lexi.

'We're at the taverna now, sweetheart,' Emma said, gazing at her daughter fondly. Lexi looked adorable. She wore a baby-blue T-shirt with 'I'm Gorgeous' printed on it and matching pedal pushers dotted with ladybirds.

'Ah,' cried the meeter and greeter. 'Good evening, beautiful lady.' And he bowed to Lexi, taking her hand and leading her to a prime position.

Emma beamed. Everywhere they went with Lexi she was met with smiles and admiration. And if there were tears, a dozen macho men would come running up to divert her, beating the women by a short head.

This was their favourite restaurant. Lexi could watch the

ponies go by and wave at them while she waited to eat, nearly falling off the balcony in the process.

Not that entertainment was lacking. Almost immediately the waiter brought the menus, plus a paper turkey for Lexi, whose fantail could be opened and closed repeatedly. Till it broke, and the vigilant waiter brought her another. And later, Lexi's ice-cream pudding managed somehow to support not only a paper parasol and flag, but a sparkler as well.

Such simple things give pleasure, Emma thought, gazing at her daughter's ecstatic face. For her, a sparkler. For me, seeing my child is happy.

After their meal they strolled along the beach arm in arm by the calm indigo sea, with Lexi perched atop Leon's shoulders. Emma was deeply content. Every night in Leon's arms she saw a greater fondness in his eyes. It was almost like the old days.

But not quite. He hadn't given himself fully to her—and wouldn't, till she was cleared of all her imagined crimes. Soon she must talk to him about the innocent part she played. And she could only hope that he'd believe her.

'Haven't seen that before.'

She followed Leon's gaze to an unlit children's playground, lurking in the dark with just the moonlight illuminating it.

'Whoopee!' she cried, breaking away with Lexi and running to the slide.

'Kids,' called Leon scornfully after them.

'That's us,' she said, unabashed.

The two of them came down the slide squealing and Leon put aside his superior male act and joined in. It was all very childish and silly but Emma found herself laughing more than she had for a very long time.

In the half-dark—which somehow made it all funnier—they sampled the swings, the roundabout and a rocker then the see-saw, laughing hysterically when Leon's weight stranded Emma and Lexi high in mid-air.

Gasping for breath and clutching aching stomachs, they walked back to the car, with Lexi chatting nineteen to the dozen.

'Lovely day, lovely evening,' Emma said dreamily as they drove back.

Alerted by the sudden silence from Lexi, Leon looked in the driving mirror and smiled. 'She's asleep,' he murmured fondly. 'How about just you and me having a meal out to-morrow night?'

'You only want to play on the slide without Lexi squealing in your ear,' she teased.

'I thought we'd go upmarket,' he said with a chuckle. 'Somewhere elegant where we can be grown up and you can wear that green dress that makes my knees tremble.'

She was secretly thrilled to know that. 'Don't choose any-thing on the menu that requires a steady hand then,' she advised.

'I think I can control myself.' He gave her a hot glance. 'Till we get in the car.'

'I'm too old for back seats.' She sniffed.

'It reclines.'

'It would.'

'Here we are, my darling,' he said softly. 'Home.'

'Home,' she repeated, awash with love.

The next day was spent on a nearby beach, searching for crabs under rocks and fishing off a small jetty. Lexi loved the sea urchins that lurked like dark black blobs in the sea, and she never seemed to tire of watching the mullet and bream and wrasse swimming lazily by beneath their dangling feet.

Donika, the caretaker's wife, was now a firm favourite with Lexi and she had agreed to babysit for the evening. When Emma and Leon were ready they went to Lexi's room to read the bed-time story and say goodnight.

'Oh.' Lexi gasped, looking at Emma in awe. *'Poli oraya!'*

'*Efharisto*,' Emma said, thanking her. And surveyed Leon, a feast for the eyes in his perfectly tailored oatmeal jacket, white open-neck shirt and biscuit trousers. 'Leon's beautiful too, isn't he?'

He went pink and said something about choosing a story. But she noticed that when she and Leon sat on either side of Lexi, her daughter kept glancing up at them both and stroking their arms contentedly.

'You're quiet,' Leon observed, when they were on their way to the restaurant.

Emma turned shining eyes to him. 'I was thinking how happy I am,' she said softly. 'You can't imagine how much pleasure it gives me, to be with you and Lexi.'

Yes, he could, Leon thought. And yet their growing intimacy as a family carried with it a bitter-sweetness. More than anything he wanted to help Emma to prove her innocence. Only then would his friends and relations accept her, and only when her reputation was clear could she be truly happy.

He reached out a hand and held hers briefly. 'I'm glad. I'd give you the world if I could,' he said huskily.

'I'll settle for a *souvlaki*,' she said, but her eyes were warm and she leaned her head on his shoulder in a gesture of affection.

It was his favourite restaurant, high on a hill above Zante town, overlooking the sweep of the bay. From the vine-covered terrace where they sat they could see the whole town laid out before them, its lights gleaming in the sultry night.

In the background a man was singing *Kantathes*, the love songs of the island. Emma looked more beautiful than he'd ever seen her. He could hardly take his eyes off her and all the time emotion was swirling inside him, depleting his appetite. They held hands across the table and he marvelled at the love in her sparkling eyes.

He kissed Emma's hand. 'Would you like a brandy, or port, or a coffee?'

Her face glowed in the candlelight and his breath caught at her vulnerability. He didn't want her to be hurt, to be unhappy.

'Let's go home,' she whispered.

As they drove off, he felt his heart fill up. He had to help her. It was obvious to him that she was innocent of fraud—she was far too honest for that. He looked at her, singing softly beside him, and wanted desperately to make her life perfect.

'Emma, tell me again,' he said urgently, 'how your job as financial director was arranged.' The happiness in her face was erased in a flash. Her hands twisted in her lap. 'Help me to understand,' he said. 'Start at the beginning so it's clear in my mind.'

Her mouth pursed and then she began. 'After marrying Taki, I was very busy, working all hours as a financial assistant in an insurance company. I didn't have much spare time. Taki said he wanted me to be the financial director for the Kyriakis bank and I told him it was impossible. He explained I could get a huge salary for doing nothing and he could easily do the work for me. It was a very common arrangement between a husband and wife. He got me to sign a document which I read—and it all seemed above-board. I had no reason not to trust him. He brought other papers for me to sign later, which he said were virtually the same as the first document so I just put my name at the bottom as he suggested. I know it was stupid and I should have read them, but he was so tetchy, so I did what he asked, even when I'd given up work to look after Lexi when she was born. I had to trust him. It was a family business, and all the profits were going to him anyway.'

He frowned. 'But there's no evidence of any kind to back up your side of the story?'

'None that my defence could come up with,' she said dolefully.

'There must have been files, accounts—'

'Apparently when the Inland Revenue swooped, the office had been stripped clean.' She hesitated. 'Leon, I know you won't like hearing this, but it looks to me that Taki knew he was in trouble and had taken steps to hide the evidence. He was certainly in an awful mood the fortnight before. Violent, drunk... That's when I said I wanted a divorce. And he was out all hours of the night.' She sighed. 'He could have burned the books or thrown them in the river. And then a week before the Revenue descended, he was killed, as you know.'

'He rang me a few days before his death,' Leon said in a low tone. 'He told me about the divorce and said he was resigning his post at the bank. He was coming home, and asked me to—'

God. He was a fool. Sharp and clear, an image came into his head. The container of Taki's effects, shipped out *before* the Revenue's investigation. He swore loudly and put his foot on the accelerator.

'Leon!' she protested. 'What are you doing?'

'Sorry.' He eased off a little but stared fixedly ahead, desperate to get back. 'Taki's things are in the house.'

Her gasp told him that she knew what he was thinking. They were both silent and tense. He took a short cut and thistles slapped against the sides of the car as he negotiated the narrow lane. Never had the journey seemed so far.

Gripping the wheel, he tried to concentrate on the road but it was difficult. Bubbling up came wild hopes that tempted him to put his foot down and scream around the roads as if the hounds of hell were on his tail.

'Deal with Donika,' he called, slewing to a halt outside the house and leaping from the car.

His heart was in his mouth as his quick stride swallowed the ground, the steps, hall, stairs...

'Please let something be here,' he muttered, reaching the door to Taki's bedroom. It was a chance. Thin and wild, but nothing more. A friend of his had unpacked the container and he'd never stepped foot in the large suite of rooms. He flung open the door and stood stock-still in amazement.

Inside, it was like Aladdin's cave. Antique furniture was crammed into the room together with silk rugs, Lalique *objets d'art*, art deco clocks and figurines and oil paintings. Impatiently he scanned the expensive clothes, electronic equipment and luxury items. His brother had lived well. A shiver went down his spine. Perhaps too well.

He could have kicked himself. If he'd only come in, and seen all this, maybe he might have wondered how Taki had acquired all these goods. And he might have done a little detective work of his own.

His gaze alighted on a stack of boxes and files piled against the wall. For a moment he stared, unable to believe his brother's deviousness. And then he clambered over a heap of designer jackets and with shaking hands he began to open the boxes, hurling papers aside when they proved to be useless.

'Oh, my God!' he heard Emma say.

'Donika? Lexi?' he enquired curtly, scanning a document.

'All fine. Let me help, Leon,' she cried, scrambling to join him.

'It's got to be here, got to be!' he exclaimed, ripping open another box. She was looking at him oddly and he paused. 'What?'

'You care,' she said gently. 'You want me to be innocent.'

'Of course I do,' he yelled, frantically scything through the contents.

'Why?'

'Because I love you, of course, you...' Had he said that? He blinked, suddenly still. He grinned at her. 'I love you,' he crowed and swept her into his arms.

'Oh, Leon.' She sighed, when they came up for air.

'I love you,' he said in delight, unable to stop himself. 'Love you,' he yelled. 'I do. I really do.'

Emma giggled. 'No need to sound so surprised. And now

let's seal that subtle declaration by proving I'm innocent,' she suggested excitedly.

They fell on the boxes with renewed enthusiasm. And then he found the account books which had been missing. Two sets. All in Taki's hand. Letters from Taki, rearranging pensions and selling off shares and then details of a Swiss bank account containing more money than Taki could ever have earned.

Leon was appalled. There was enough evidence here to have damned his brother. When they'd finished checking the last document, they had found nothing, not one thing that showed Emma had ever been a part of her husband's fraudulent scam.

Dusty and dishevelled, Leon sank to the floor, shaken by the shame and the awful realisation that his brother had caused unbelievable suffering to the woman he loved.

'My brother,' he whispered, white with shock. 'My own brother!'

CHAPTER TWELVE

EMMA took him by the hand and led him to his bathroom where she gently removed his clothes and hers, and showered the dust and memories from both their bodies.

'How can you ever forgive me?' he asked passionately.

'It was Taki, not you,' she said soothingly.

'But I didn't believe you—'

'I was fooled by him at first, too,' she reminded him. 'He was miles away from you—how could you know how his hatred of you had turned his mind? He always said he wanted to be richer than you are. He found a way of achieving that. Besides, I was the one under investigation. There was nothing to point the finger at him. That's why I was so frustrated. I couldn't prove my innocence. He'd been too clever.'

Leon seemed to be in a total state of shock, just apologising and blaming himself for the misery she'd suffered. So she dried him and led him to bed where he lay on his back, his muscles tensed alarmingly while he stared hazily at the ceiling.

'You lost your reputation, your job, your freedom and your child,' he said hoarsely.

All that seemed so long ago. Water under the bridge. And the future was looking just wonderful. She smiled.

'But I won a lot more. And I'll get the rest back, won't I?' Lovingly she kissed his shoulder.

'I can't forgive myself,' he muttered.

'If I can, so can you,' she said with a laugh. 'Leon, I'm happy. Ecstatic. You love me. There's only one more thing I want.'

He rolled over, his eyes glistening with unshed tears. 'Cup of tea?' he said jerkily, attempting a joke.

Emma smiled. 'Lexi, you nut case. And,' she murmured, sliding her hand over his chest, 'something else, for the time being.'

He kissed her, his mouth desperate on hers. For a while he was like a tiger unleashed, his passion white-hot, each kiss more torrid than the one before. And gradually, soothed by her languorous movements and slow, seductive caresses, he grew less frantic and more tender.

'I love you,' he whispered, his voice cracking with emotion.

'I love you back,' she said in a purring voice, stretching her feline body luxuriously.

His mouth descended and she gave herself to him, utterly content.

They had been building up to the big moment all day when Leon would tell Lexi that Emma was her mother. And now they all settled themselves on the sofa and Leon put on the video for them all to watch.

'That is Emma,' he said, as the picture came up. 'I knew her a long time ago. She was my best friend. I loved her a lot.'

Sitting between them both, Lexi watched with enjoyment, laughing when Emma fell into the pond. 'Again, please,' she cried. So it was rewound and played once more.

Leon turned the television off. 'Emma knew your daddy, remember?' he murmured, cuddling Lexi close. Emma held her breath. 'Sweetheart,' Leon said gently, taking Lexi's small hands in his, 'do you like Emma?'

Emma quivered as her daughter flung her a big smile.

'Lots,' Lexi said, clapping her hands.

Emma felt a huge lump of emotion clogging her throat. This was the moment she'd been waiting for. Leon was clearly nervous. He swallowed.

'Lexi, you are a big girl now,' he said flatteringly. 'Big enough for me to tell you something special.'

Lexi's eyes grew enormous as Leon took a deep breath. Emma held hers, every nerve in her body screwed up in apprehension as Leon continued.

'Sweetheart, you are a very lucky girl.' He stroked Lexi's soft cheek and kissed it while Emma felt her stomach knot up unbearably. 'Emma,' he said gently, 'is your mummy.'

Lexi blinked at Leon and then up at Emma who sat with tears in her eyes.

'Yes. I am your mummy, sweetheart,' she said huskily.

At Lexi's wriggle, Leon released his arms and the little girl slid off his lap. Emma smiled shakily and opened her arms to her beloved child.

But Lexi stood frowning. And then she ran out into the garden.

There was an appalled silence. Emma couldn't speak, couldn't think and had become frozen like a statue in her seat. She felt Leon get up and move to the open door, his feet sounding heavy and slow on the tiled floor.

Desolation swept through her. She stared blankly into space, unable to believe what had happened.

'She's talking to the doll you gave her,' Leon said, from somewhere far away.

'Calling it Mama?' she choked.

'Darling,' he whispered and she knew she'd been right. 'Come here,' he begged. 'I can't let Lexi out of my sight. Come and sit with me.'

She couldn't. There was no life, no energy in her body. 'I feel sick,' she mumbled, and rushed off to the bathroom.

Wiping her face later, she looked at her reflection in the mirror and wondered where the pale, tragic-eyed woman had come from. It seemed that the happiness of the past few days counted as nothing. She knew that was ridiculous, that she and Leon were made for one another and would be lovers for the rest of their lives, but...

'Oh, Lexi!' she moaned.

Suddenly she wanted Leon. With a sob, she ran out to him,

absorbed his groan of utter relief and the frantic worry on his face, and hurled herself into the welcoming circle of his arms.

He rocked her like a child. 'She'll get the hang of it,' he assured her. 'Give her time.'

'And if not?' She snuffled into his shoulder.

'She will. She cares for you. Hey, darling, sometimes I'm jealous of you two girls giggling together.'

She wouldn't be cheered up. She felt even too numb to cry now. The ravages of the past few minutes had gone deeper than tears. She feared that she might never claim her daughter.

Leon eased her to the top step. They sat with their arms around each other watching Lexi whispering to her doll. Leon got out his handkerchief and blew his nose loudly. Miserably Emma looked at him and saw that tears were trickling from his eyes and he was blinking, trying to stop them before she noticed.

'Oh, my darling,' she whispered, laying her head on his shoulder.

He kissed her forehead. 'I love you so much,' he said brokenly. 'I want Lexi to love you too—'

He muttered irritably as the phone set up its insistent ringing. 'Cursed thing! I'll put it onto the answer-machine—'

'No. You answer it,' she whispered.

Dropping a quick kiss on her head, he left her. She didn't dare go into the garden. Lexi might be upset if she did. Emma bit her lip hard. She never imagined she'd ever be jealous of a doll in a bikini, she thought, trying to raise her own spirits. It didn't work. The coil of nausea lurked like bitter gall in her stomach.

My child, she thought, tormenting herself. My baby! She had come so far, fought so hard and yet a tiny little girl had shattered all her dearest hopes.

'Lexi,' she mumbled, consumed with misery. She pressed

a hand to her aching heart and tried to believe that it would be all right, one day.

And suddenly she saw that Lexi was scrambling up onto a low drystone wall—something she'd been told never to do. Before she could call out, Lexi was on top of it and had slipped.

Emma ran like the wind, her spine freezing at the blood-curdling scream. Lexi got to her feet and began to run to her, wailing at the top of her voice.

'Mummy. Mummy!'

'Oh-h-h!' Emma shuddered as her arms enfolded her daughter, their tears mingling. 'What is it, darling? Where does it hurt?' she asked with a sob.

'I f-f-fell.' Lexi wept, pointing to her knee.

'It's all right,' she said shakily. 'Mummy will kiss it better.' Emma bent and kissed the grubby little knee, tasting a tiny smidgen of blood. My daughter, she thought, her heart singing as she hugged the snuffling child. My darling daughter.

'What's wrong?' came Leon's anxious voice.

And Emma didn't mind when Lexi slithered from her grasp and ran to him. Blurry-eyed she rose, feeling she could weep for joy.

'And Mummy kissed it better!' Lexi was saying with all the pride of a hero discussing his war wound.

'Uh-huh.' Leon's voice cracked completely. He glanced up at Emma and cleared his throat. 'That's what mummies do,' he said softly.

'I said to dolly,' Lexi said, 'my mummy has come.'

'I see. That was kind,' Emma said.

'Can you be my daddy?' Lexi asked earnestly, as Leon dabbed at her knee with a handkerchief.

He smiled. 'I would like that,' he said fervently. 'Emma?'

'Need you ask?' she whispered, feeling far too weak to stand unaided.

Shaking with emotion, Leon swept them both into his embrace: the two people he loved most on earth. He felt quite delirious.

'This is an odd place and an even odder moment for a proposal, but I can do the bended knee and flowers and wine later. Just now,' he whispered to Emma, 'I have to know if you'll marry me. I love you with all my heart. I want to be with you for ever. Please say yes,' he urged fervently.

'Oh, Leon, as if I'd ever refuse you. Yes, yes,' she said breathily and, overjoyed, he kissed her.

'Do mummy and daddies,' said Lexi horribly loud in his ear, 'do kisses too?'

He dropped a quick peck on the baby cheek. 'Oh, yes,' he said, feeling like shouting with happiness. 'Lots.'

Emma laughed. 'I love you both so much,' she said breathlessly.

It was dreadfully late by the time the excited Lexi had gone to sleep. Emma sat on the terrace with Leon, curled up in the big cane chair with him, and listening to the frogs pulsing in the background while the bats laid on an aerial display. Somewhere in the distance she could hear the electronic call of the scops owl, and the occasional bark of a dog echoed across the peaceful valley.

'Got any champagne on ice?' she asked casually.

He gave a wicked chuckle. 'Two bottles. One for each of us.' His mouth met hers in a long, thorough kiss.

Emma felt drunk already. 'Seems a waste to pour it down our throats,' she murmured and, encouraged by his passionate growl, led the way indoors.

CALL THE ONES YOU LOVE OVER THE HOLIDAYS!

Save $25 off future book purchases when you buy any four Harlequin® or Silhouette® books in October, November and December 2001,

PLUS

receive a phone card good for 15 minutes of long-distance calls to anyone you want in North America!

WHAT AN INCREDIBLE DEAL!

Just fill out this form and attach 4 proofs of purchase (cash register receipts) from October, November and December 2001 books, and Harlequin Books will send you a coupon booklet worth a total savings of $25 off future purchases of Harlequin® and Silhouette® books, AND a 15-minute phone card to call the ones you love, anywhere in North America.

Please send this form, along with your cash register receipts as proofs of purchase, to:
In the USA: Harlequin Books, P.O. Box 9057, Buffalo, NY 14269-9057
In Canada: Harlequin Books, P.O. Box 622, Fort Erie, Ontario L2A 5X3
Cash register receipts must be dated no later than December 31, 2001.
Limit of 1 coupon booklet and phone card per household.
Please allow 4-6 weeks for delivery.

I accept your offer! Enclosed are 4 proofs of purchase. Please send me my coupon booklet and a 15-minute phone card:

Name: _____

Address: _____ City: _____

State/Prov.: _____ Zip/Postal Code: _____

Account Number (if available): _____

---

097 KJB DAGL
PHQ4013